MY SEXY RIVAL

STARS IN THEIR EYES DUET (BOOK TWO)

LAUREN BLAKELY

ALSO BY LAUREN BLAKELY

Big Rock Series

Big Rock

Mister O

Well Hung

Full Package

Joy Ride

Hard Wood

One Love Series dual-POV Standalones

The Sexy One

The Only One

The Hot One

Sports Romance

Most Valuable Playboy

Most Likely to Score

Standalones

The Knocked Up Plan

Stud Finder

The V Card

Stars In Their Eyes Duet

My Charming Rival

My Sexy Rival

The No Regrets Series

The Thrill of It

The Start of Us

Every Second With You

The Seductive Nights Series

First Night (Julia and Clay, prequel novella)

Night After Night (Julia and Clay, book one)

After This Night (Julia and Clay, book two)

One More Night (Julia and Clay, book three)

A Wildly Seductive Night (Julia and Clay novella, book 3.5)

The Joy Delivered Duet

Nights With Him (A standalone novel about Michelle and Jack)

Forbidden Nights (A standalone novel about Nate and Casey)

The Sinful Nights Series

Sweet Sinful Nights

Sinful Desire

Sinful Longing

Sinful Love

The Fighting Fire Series

Burn For Me (Smith and Jamie)

Melt for Him (Megan and Becker)

Consumed By You (Travis and Cara)

The Jewel Series

A two-book sexy contemporary romance series

The Sapphire Affair

The Sapphire Heist

AUTHOR'S NOTE

Author's Note: This book was originally released as part of Stars in Their Eyes in 2014. It has been revised and repackaged into a duet for a new readership. If you previously read Stars in Their Eyes, you don't need to read this book. If you've read My Charming Rival, then you'll definitely want to read on to learn what happens next! This is book 2 in a duet!

1

William

The noise from the Cessna rattled the sky as the dark blue jet hit air at the far end of the runway. Being a guy, it was nearly impossible for me to tear my eyes away from the plane as it began soaring. When I was younger, I had once imagined I'd be a fighter pilot because that is one of the most badass professions a guy can be. For now, I had to focus on turning my under-the-table part-time private eye gig into a full-time-working-visa job.

I forced myself to look away from the plane as it stole through the crystal blue sky.

"This baby looks good to go," James said, patting the side of the silver helicopter on the tarmac of the Santa Monica airport.

"Yes, sir. I'll be all ready for Saturday," the

chopper pilot said, giving James a crisp salute. "And I will be sure to keep a good distance so as not to disturb the festivities."

"Excellent," James said, and I noticed he was personable with the pilot. Maybe it was just family he saved his douche-y side for. He clapped the pilot he'd hired on the back. The helicopter was part of the security plans for Saturday, circling above Ojai Ranch as the eye in the sky. The pilot's job was also to blend in, which meant make very little noise while somehow circling above the grounds for the whole event. A fine line to toe, and since James was a thorough fellow, he'd wanted to stop by the Santa Monica airport for a triple check.

"Your turn. I've got three minutes, kid," he said, crooking his finger at me to follow him across the tarmac, his bald spot gleaming in the sun like a bull's-eye. "Tell me everything you've learned so far." Too busy for even a phone call, he'd told me to meet him here to give him the update on the case he'd assigned me—I called it *Days of Our Lenses, An Inside Tale of the Paparazzo Secrets*. Well, that's what I called it in my head. When speaking to my uncle, I simply gave him the specific details his client had asked for, and made a mental note to procure a fabulous thank you gift for Jess, since her insider information was the reason I still had this part-time job.

"And hookups?" he asked. "Those are usually just a tip from someone in the know?"

I nodded as the cool air of the terminal whooshed past us. James walked purposefully, taking long strides across the industrial carpet on his way to his car in the parking lot.

"Yes. That seems to be the case," I said, careful not to reveal details of who we'd staked out last night. Besides, James had never asked for those particulars— he just needed to know the how and why.

"What about gym shots?"

"I'll get more info on those," I said as he reached the gate to the lot.

"Yeah, you do that. Because I need more," he said, tapping his finger against my shoulder in a patronizing manner.

I drew a deep, fueling breath. "Thank you, James. I'd love to keep doing this if this is helpful to you. Do you think you'd be able to bring me on for a full-time position and sponsor my visa?"

God, I sounded like a fucking beggar and I hated it. But I had no choice. I'd been moonlighting for him for three months now and I was dying to know if he was seriously considering me for a job or was dangling me along.

He lowered his shades and peered at me over the top of the tinted frames, only half his eyes visible. "Get me more details and we'll see then and only then. I've got this wedding on my mind and I can't think beyond that to your little employment situation."

He opened his car door and took off.

I flipped him the bird once his car was out of sight.

As I tracked down my bike, a small round of guilt went rat-a-tat-tat against my chest, like a mobster's gun in an old-school crime flick. Yes, Jess was on the guest list, and sure, James had never expressly forbade photographers. But even though he was a dick, I was sneaking her into the wedding.

Except sneaking her in was the price I had to pay to get the goods that he wanted.

The goods that just might keep me in the country.

As I gunned the engine and drove to see Jess, I wondered if staying in the United States was worth all this effort.

Jess

I ducked behind the fern, and a tumble of questions scurried through my head, as I registered who I was looking at — Keats, his older brother, and the *other guy*. I recognized *the other guy* from my flash cards.

The embattled teen actor who'd decked a hotel clerk. The bleached blond with the broody brown eyes. Jenner "I Want a Room With a View on my Planet" Davies.

The three of them were all laughing and toasting.

Why would Jenner Davies meet with the owner of a photo agency? J.P. never ran around with stars and the people his photogs snapped pictures of. It would be the equivalent of a dog actively courting fleas. The fleas did their work quietly and in the distance, but never letting on they were setting up camp on the canines. Yes, I'd just compared J.P. to a flea, but I knew he'd be okay with the metaphor because he understood the roles, the system, the way things were supposed to work. Stars did not consort with photographers.

And why was Keats's older brother there? The other guy had the same ruddy cheeks and the same tiny little nose, as if they'd both procured rhinoplasty from an identical mold.

Even as these questions flooded my brain, I didn't let them paralyze me. My shooter's instincts had kicked in, as I crouched by the plant, grabbed my camera, and began snapping pictures of Jenner. My main employer would happily take an unposed picture of Jenner Davies. J.P. would prefer it to the plethora of staged shots of Jenner glad-handing with recipients of his pre-planned charitable work. Plus, a random star sighting like this would earn me a few more bucks than a playground shot.

They didn't notice me, and the maître d' didn't, either, or else his palm had already been greased by many a photo agency to look the other way. After I'd snapped enough shots, I tucked my camera in my backpack and retraced my steps to the bathroom, this time on a dual mission. I retrieved my toothbrush and toothpaste, then ducked into a stall and quickly downloaded the shots, sending them off to J.P. from my laptop along with a note that said *Special Delivery: Just a little surprise for you. I know how you like them unposed.*

A few dollar signs flashed before my eyes. The money would be good, and so would his reaction. I couldn't wait to hear about J.P's sure-to-be-gleeful delight when he discovered the unexpected photos.

Forty-five seconds later I was rewarded with a reply: *Bring that digital baby to papa. Selling these now!*

Pride from a job well done suffused me as I left the restaurant unnoticed, yet again. I'd need to research Keats Wharton in more detail later this afternoon, but I reminded myself that whatever Keats was doing with Jenner Davies didn't impact me. It couldn't impact me, right? Because the check, so to speak, had already cleared.

A few feet away from the restaurant, I spotted a light blue Vespa, idling on the Promenade. On that blue Vespa was Flash herself, shooting away, snapping the same photos of Jenner.

Satisfaction curled through me as I watched her.

She was good, that girl, but this time I'd been first to shoot. That also meant I was hair's breadth lucky. Had Flash been a minute earlier, she might have spotted me, and figured out The Dog Savior was really a paparazzo. I'd need to be as incognito as possible before the wedding. For my sake, and William's.

His name alone sent a rush of sweet tingles across my chest as I remembered last night and the words he'd said in Italian that I didn't understand. But they had sounded undeniably sexy falling from his lips. My skin turned hot as I recalled his kisses, the way he touched me, the connection between our bodies.

I swung by my parents' house to leash up Jennifer, and as I worked through my volunteer shift at the hospital, I didn't push aside the memories of last night. Instead, I let them skip happily through my brain, warming my body, keeping me company, until the clock ticked closer to William time. When my shift ended, I headed for the exit, the dog in a neat heel by my side, wagging her tail when she spotted Helen, who ran the program, rounding the corner.

"Hey. Did you hear there's going to be an *It's Raining Men, Part II?*"

"Thankfully, Hollywood is finally learning that male strippers are a big draw at the box office."

"I'll be at the theater on opening night with my one dollar bills ready to toss at the screen," Helen said, patting the dog and chatting more as she walked toward the lobby with me. William was waiting by the door, his jeans and T-shirt hugging him in all the right places, showing off his toned arms without making him look like a show-off. He *was* casual and cool; he didn't try to appear that way. He simply was that way, from how he dressed to his laid-back grin. He flashed a smile when he saw me, and my belly flipped, then flopped, then flipped again with butterflies. He was so handsome, and so delectable, and he was here for me. As soon as Helen noticed him, the clipboard she was holding slipped from her hands to the floor with a loud clang. William bent down to retrieve it, quickly handing it back to her.

Gallant William.

"Helen, this is my friend William," I said, and William extended his hand.

"It's a pleasure to meet you, Helen," he said, sounding so proper, and it occurred to me how that was yet another side to him. Funny, smart, and polite. Manners ruled.

"I assure you, the pleasure is all mine," she said with a wink, then said in a loud stage whisper. "He's hot. Have double the fun for me, please."

"Helen!"

"Get out of here, Jess. You're only young once," she said, then tra-la-la-ed down the hall and away from me.

"I like your dog," William said, as he petted Jennifer on the head, then turned his attention to the Great Dane–bullmastiff mix who was a gentle giant. "Well, hello, Jennifer. Aren't you gorgeous?"

Her tail thumped against the floor.

"Don't think you can work your little British magic on the dog, too," I said. "She is immune to accents."

"But you're not," he said, wiggling an eyebrow.

"Evidently not."

As we left, I shrugged an apology for Helen. "Sorry about Helen's sauciness. She kind of has a thing for hot young guys."

Once outside, he grabbed my waist and pulled me in close, his dark gray eyes fixed on me. The way he stared at me like he wanted me made me molten. My knees felt wobbly from his heady gaze. Those tingles racing through my body an hour ago? They had nothing on the handsprings my stomach was executing now. "What about your friend, Claire Tinsley? Does she have a thing for hot young guys? Especially the ones who speak many languages and catch volleyballs in their bare hands?"

"I thought we already made that clear," I said, threading my free hand through his hair and planting a quick, hot kiss on his lips that soon became a deep, slow, intense kiss…the kind that melted me from the inside out and turned everything it touched into gold. His kisses made my head so hazy and my body so warm that I swore they could convince me of anything—the sky is purple, the sun rises in the west, and chocolate is calorie-free. All of that felt true in the way he kissed, turning my world inside out and upside down. All my ambitions, all my plans slinked away in the glide of his lips, the insistent explorations of his tongue, because all I wanted now was to spend the day in this cocoon of his sweet, sultry kisses under the sun.

I broke apart because my leg was wet. Jennifer was licking my calf, her way of saying *time's up, lady*. She batted her big brown eyes at me and nudged my leg once more.

"I need to walk her back to my parents' house before we head out," I said, glancing at her jowly face.

"I'll walk with you." He reached for my hand. "I hope you know I adore kissing you."

Kisses with him were spectacular. Add in his flirty, swoony words, chase them with a touch of naughtiness, and I was quickly sliding down the path to a frazzled brain. Like a marble rattling down a chute, he was poised to knock my carefully controlled life out of orbit.

The only saving grace was that his future was uncertain. He'd be leaving the country in two months if he didn't land a job with a company that would sponsor his work visa. I held onto the possibility that we would never become more than a brief interlude our senior year of college. Neither one of us had the bandwidth for a relationship, or even for more regular dating. There were built-in barriers to protect me from falling.

I could erect more, though, just to keep my untamed heart and mind safe as safe could be.

"We should go," I mumbled even though I wanted to sing, to shout, to tell everyone that I adored kissing him, too.

So. Very. Much.

2

Jess

William parked himself in a chair at the corner café next to J.P.'s office. "Back in five. I'll tell your former short-lived employer you said hi," I said as I opened the door to the building. I needed to get paid, and get the afternoon assignments.

"Yes. Please do that," he said as he pulled out his iPad to work on homework while waiting for me.

"You liked my surprise pic?" I asked J.P. as I entered his dark and dimly lit confines.

"You made my day with it," he said, swiveling the screen around to show me where the shot of Jenner at lunch had landed—the website *On the Surface*.

"Good. Now make my day, J.P. Why was Jenner Davies having lunch with a guy who runs a photo agency?"

"Huh?"

"The guy in the photo," I said, pointing to Keats on the computer screen on his desk. "The guy he's having lunch with."

J.P. stabbed his meaty finger against the other guy in the picture, the one who looked like a carbon copy of Keats.

"That guy," J.P. said, gesturing to the older of the small-nosed brothers, "is Jenner Davies's publicist."

My eyebrows knit together as I tried to process what he'd just said. "What?"

"Name is Wordsworth Wharton," J.P. said and laughed loudly, then rolled his eyes. "Can you believe it? What am I going to learn next? That his brother is named Keats?"

It was a rhetorical question. Even so, I whispered *yes*. But I still didn't move a muscle; I sat in the rickety wooden chair by his desk, with some kind of strange, unexpected shock on my features. Keats's older brother was Jenner's publicist, and the trio of them had seemed immensely pleased. A sense of unease rolled through me, as if the joke was on me, only I had no clue what it was.

J.P. stared hard at me as if I were two puzzle pieces he couldn't quite align. "Jess, what's the big deal? Actors have lunch with their publicists all the time."

Right. I couldn't let on that Jenner wasn't *just* having lunch with his publicist. Jenner Davies was having lunch with his publicist and also his publicist's younger brother who *happened* to run a rival photo agency that had *happened* to contract for shots of a secret tryst between a young actress and a married director. I had inside information, but the information didn't add up, so I plastered on my best game face as I tried to mentally connect the dots between Jenner and the poetically named pair of brothers. Maybe they were all buddies. Maybe Wordsworth was helping Keats grow his business. Maybe their get-together was simply the next item on Keats's agenda for the day.

But that moment of laughter when they all seemed to be in on the same joke weighed on me.

Not wanting to be surprised again, I made a mental note to add faces of publicists to my flash cards, because I hadn't recognized Jenner's publicist.

I shifted gears. "I've got a lead on the wedding. Looks like I might be able to get in," I told him. I didn't want to promise too much too soon.

"Tell me more." J.P. licked his lips in that way he did when he was getting excited for a shot, and the greenbacks it would bring. "Because I heard from someone at WAM that the ceremony starts at two on Saturday," he said, referring to the biggest talent agency in town that happened to rep Chelsea Knox, Bradley Bowman, and both Veronica and Riley Belle.

His source at WAM had gotten the time right. That was good corroboration. Inadvertent, but good. The fact that his source knew the correct time also meant that details on the wedding were starting to leak out, so I'd need to keep the ones I knew close to the vest. I didn't tell J.P. where the ceremony was really going to be. J.P. had unleashed what he had presumed was the competition on me earlier in the week in the form of William; I wasn't going to disclose the most precious detail I possessed, even though J.P. was good to me.

"I know someone on security detail," I said, once again keeping my cards to myself. "Says he can get me in. All I need is a fake ID. Got any idea where in this town I can get one of those bad boys on short notice?" I asked with a wink.

He held his arms in the air, the sign of victory. "I knew eventually you'd cave, Jess! Damn, I impress myself."

"Yeah, preen later. Anyway, I need it tomorrow."

He raised an eyebrow. "Fast turnaround? That'll cost you double."

"You're not honestly going to charge me for a fake ID so I can get into a wedding and deliver *you* exclusively a shot of the most sought-after photo Hollywood has seen in years?"

"Just kidding." He rose and walked over to the one plywood wall in his office that didn't have posters or frames of his greatest photographic hits on it, then yanked down a rolling white blind.

I handed him my camera, stood in front of the blind, and gave a scowl.

"C'mon. Say cheese for the fake DMV."

"Cheese," I said as he snapped a picture. Then I remembered a key detail that rendered this photo shoot moot. "Crap. I'm going to wear a wig on Saturday. I can't use this shot."

"What color wig?"

"Brunette probably. Why? Got extra in your drawer?"

"Yeah. I make fake IDs," he said, as if it was obvious to anyone that he'd keep a stash of wigs close at hand. "'Course I have extra."

I contemplated putting on a wig that someone else had worn. I pictured getting lice. I knew better than to wear someone else's headgear.

"If I send you a picture later of me in the wig I'm going to wear, can you just Photoshop it in front of the background? I mean, you were just going to Photoshop me anyway in front of the California license background, right?"

"Get it to me by eight. I've got a hot date, and I'm going off the clock tonight."

"I'll send it to you by then."

"All right. Now do you think you can get your pretty little butt out of here and take some pictures for me over on Melrose?" he said, rattling off the names of several TV stars whose assistants planned to take them shopping today.

"I'm on it," I said. Besides, there was a wig shop on Melrose where I could grab Claire Tinsley's 'do. After all, I had a wedding to crash in less than forty-eight hours.

I found William at the table outside, looking cool and casual and completely kissable. My stomach twisted in knots with wanting him, and then once more with wishing I didn't want him so much.

I tried to tell myself he wasn't the guy I was falling

for. He was only my partner-in-crime, and nothing more.

But the rush of heat in my veins, and the fluttering in my chest, said otherwise.

I proceeded to share with him all that I'd learned about Keats and Wordsworth, hoping the focus on work would distract me from matters of the heart.

3

William

A font of celebrity insight, Jess knew everything about every star, from their relationship status, to their list of credits, to their shooting schedules. She also knew about gene structure, and biology, and cells—not that we discussed science—but I found it insanely hot that she was so smart. While I still possessed a supreme lack of knowledge about celebrities, I knew a tad more from spending the time by her side, taking notes on how she documented shopping habits of the stars in a pocket-size black-and-white notebook.

First, she hustled bracelet-shopping photos of Emily Hannigan, who had a regular role on a hospital show as a one-legged doctor, Jess informed me.

"She's on *Trauma Tonight.* And is in consideration for the Gretchen Lindstrom role on *We'll Always Have*

Paris, I read earlier today. You really don't recognize her?" she asked.

"Nope," I'd said, shaking my head. "Though it could be that the pair of limbs are throwing me off."

Next, she nabbed a shot of two mustached young actors who held hands while perusing polo shirts in a nearby shop. "How about those guys? They're all over the magazines."

I shook my head.

"They're Jim and Jack Turner-Grace. They play rival detectives on a set-in-the-seventies cable show. They fell in love on set," she explained. "I thought for sure you'd recognize them. The press loves them and so do their fans. They're about to adopt two little girls from Vietnam."

"How many times do I have to tell you, Jess? It's like you're speaking Russian."

"Because that's the only language you don't speak."

"In addition to *celebrity*."

"I'm going to pretend you didn't say that," she'd said, bumping my shoulder playfully as we left the shop. "I don't understand how you can live in this town and not be addicted to gossip."

"You're such a junkie."

"Card-carrying member."

Then, through the window of a sneaker store, she spotted the fifteen-year-old rising pop sensation Rain Storm—yes, he claimed that was his given name, a Google search on my phone revealed—who'd become a hit after several Ivy League water polo teams had performed lip syncs of his latest tune on YouTube. She snared a picture of him wearing a red plaid vest as he purchased a pair of matching red high-top sneakers.

"That's for Anaka, but I'll give it to J.P., too, because they both find Rain amusing," she said, then snapped a few more shots of other celebrities along Melrose, including one of the stars of LGO's *Lords and Ladies*, when Anaka's cousin texted her with a tip she'd just landed on their whereabouts.

"Her mom produces the show. But evidently that tip came from some hot guy. Which means Anaka and I are going to have to get the full story on her cousin's romantic situation," Jess told me as she sent the final set of shots to J.P.

Not a bad take for her for an afternoon's worth of trolling, plus I'd gleaned plenty of intel on a day in the life of a paparazzo. We were both getting something out of this partnership, and I wanted it to continue in all ways. When we were finished, I suggested we stop at the Busy Bee Eatery for a bite to eat, so we snagged a table at a diner decked out in black-and-yellow decor, matching the name.

"Now it's my turn to help you," I said, and after we ordered, I did some digging online on my iPad, quickly finding a photo of the poet brothers. They wore white linen shorts and blue button-down shirts, and smiled for the camera from the deck of a big boat floating on the water. God bless Facebook, and the ease of finding someone's life story on the site.

"I seriously cannot believe their parents really

named them Wordsworth and Keats. It's so affected," I said, as I showed her the picture of the two brothers.

As she studied it closely, I studied her. The gray T-shirt she wore fit her snugly, making her breasts look even more enticing. My eyes drifted to her curves for the thousandth time today, and my mind meandered back to last night and the memory of how soft and wonderful they'd felt in my hands. How she'd grabbed my head and pulled me in close. How her skin smelled so enticing. I shifted in the booth, grateful we were sitting down. Then I returned to the matter at hand because if I lingered on last night, I wouldn't be able to form coherent sentences.

Fortunately, any discussion of Keats and Wordsworth was a huge boner killer, so I closed the Facebook shot and returned to the unposed images Jess had captured at Rosanna's Hideout of the three guys toasting.

"Let's figure this out," I said.

"Do you think they were all toasting to the photos I took? The Riley and Avery shots that I had just handed over? Your client is a publicity shop. You must know something about how publicists operate. Do you think Jenner's publicist wanted those shots? The pictures of Riley and Avery haven't shown up on any of the gossip sites, and it's been more than four hours since he's had the pictures."

She tapped her watch to make her point. It was now five o'clock.

"They're really not anywhere?"

"I've checked everywhere. All the usual suspects,"

she said, then rattled off the names of several celebrity sites. "The pictures aren't anywhere. And they don't show up on a Google search, either, nor on a Twitter search, so they must not have been posted anywhere. It makes no sense. Why would you spend that kind of jack for photos and not get them out immediately? Those kind of pictures drive an insane amount of traffic to a website."

"It's weird," I said, contemplating the scenarios.

"It's weird?"

"Yeah. It's weird."

"That's it? It's *weird*? That's your assessment as a private detective?"

"Yeah," I said firmly. "It is weird. Weird meaning fishy. Suspicious. Not quite what it seems."

She nodded with enthusiasm. "Exactly! That's my point. So what do we do?"

"What do you want me to do? Follow Keats? Follow Wordsworth? Follow Jenner?" I asked, offering it as a joke at first, but as soon as the suggestion left my mouth, it seemed Jess and I felt the same way.

Her eyes lit up. "Actually, that's a brilliant idea."

"It is, isn't it?"

"Yes," she said, barely able to contain a grin.

"I'm like your personal PI now, right, Jess?"

"*Personal PI,*" she said in a deep TV show announcer voice. "*Premiere episode tonight at nine p.m. When our red-hot hero tries to nab a pair of poet brothers.*"

I raised an eyebrow. "Red hot?"

Her tongue darted out to lick her lips.

"You do that as if it's playful, but you look red hot, too."

The waitress arrived with my chicken sandwich and French fries and Jess's coffee and fruit cup. "Need anything else?"

"Yes, please. Some actual *food* for my friend," I said, eyeing Jess's plate of rabbit food.

"I'm fine. This is completely fine," Jess said to the waitress, who turned on her heels and walked away.

I narrowed my eyes at her plate. "I will follow the Chia Brothers with the tiny noses and matching Oxford shirts under one condition."

"What is that condition?"

"I want you to have one of these French fries," I said, leaning back against the light blue vinyl of the fifties-style booth. There was a jukebox at the edge of the table, and soda shop music played overhead.

She shook her head, and bit the corner of her lip.

"I can't," she whispered and pushed her fork through the melons and pineapple pieces. "You don't have to follow them."

This wasn't the strong, confident woman I'd gotten to know. This was another side of Jess. I sensed it was a side she didn't show anyone. It was what lurked beneath all that tough-girl armor.

I stripped all teasing from my tone, wanting to reassure her. "Hey. It's okay. You don't have to eat any fries. I'll still check out those guys for you. But you know, Jess, I have to say this. You look fantastic, and you'd look fantastic if you were this big," I said and held my hands out wide, then brought them closer together. "Or this small. What I mean is, I don't have a clue about sizes, but you look amazing now, and you'd look amazing if you ate French fries and more ice cream. And you're just cool, too. And smart. And funny. Even though you totally ride me, and hate me, and think I'm clueless for not knowing celebs. I still think you're funny and fun to hang out with, so I guess I'm a masochist."

That earned me a big grin. "I don't hate you, William. Not at all. Not in the least," she said, her pretty blue eyes locked straight on mine as she spoke.

I knew she meant it earnestly, but I couldn't resist teasing her. I steepled my fingers together. "Thank you so much for not hating me."

"You know it's not just *not* hate." Her voice was gentle, sweet even.

"All the double negatives are confusing me. Why don't you just spell it out?"

"You're fun to hang out with," she muttered, as if she were pretending it cost her something.

"I knew I could wear you down," I said, and picked up a French fry, dragged it through some ketchup, and happily ate it. She looked at the French fry with longing, blinking her eyes once then tearing her gaze away. In that moment, I understood her. Throwing away the ice cream on the beach, turning down my offer for pizza, eating only air-popped popcorn—they weren't part of her hard edge. They were real struggles. Food wasn't a struggle I knew personally, but being in Southern California for even a short while had taught me that body image was a battle for many men and women, guys and girls.

"Jess," I asked carefully. "You know you're beautiful, don't you?"

"Thank you, but that's not it."

"What is it?"

She shook her head, as if voicing her concerns would pain her. She took a deep breath then spoke. "French fries are my downfall. They're more dangerous than you. I haven't thrown up food I've eaten in more than two years, so I'm just trying to stay on the healthy-eating wagon."

"I didn't realize it was hard for you," I said, reaching across the table and lacing my fingers through hers.

She let me, her fingers curling around mine. "I don't usually talk about it. It was a while ago anyway."

"You don't talk about it because you try so hard to be so tough. But that's a tough thing, dealing with an eating disorder. And that's a huge thing to be able to move beyond it."

"The last time I did it," she said in a small voice, "it was over French fries." Then she stopped talking, dropped her face into her hands. "Ugh. I can't believe I'm talking about barfing while you're eating." For one of the first times, Jess was fragile. All that armor she wore cracked with a small fissure, and in those tiny breaks, she was letting parts of herself be shown.

I joined her on the other side of the booth, wrapping an arm around her. "Hey, it's totally okay. I swear you can't gross me out about food or anything. I didn't mean to make you feel bad by suggesting you eat a fry," I said, squeezing her shoulder gently.

"You didn't make me feel bad," she whispered in a barren voice, her face still covered with her fingers. She wasn't crying. Rather, she was embarrassed and I hated that she felt that way.

"I never should have said anything about the French fry," I said, rubbing her shoulder now with my palm.

She snorted, and it was a self-deprecating sound. Lifting her fingers from her face and raising her head, she composed herself. "You know what? It's fine. It's just a French fry. I can handle it. I'm not going to be a big baby about a French fry," she said and reached across the table to my plate to grab a fry. She bit into it as if to prove she could do it. Then she finished it, and held her arms out wide.

"There. Did it," she said, clearly mocking the momentousness of eating something that had once been far too tempting.

"And it didn't even bite back," I said, and she laughed, then looked at me.

"Thank you," she said softly. "For not mocking me."

"For being human? Never," I said, then turned serious again. "How long were you bulimic?"

"Through most of high school. I never told anyone, but Anaka figured it out and was pretty supportive. She even took me to a support group, and that helped me to really deal with it. It was never about food. It was always about control, and I felt so out of control starting in high school when my dad's company went under and my college fund went kaput. So, controlling food felt like the only thing I could manage. But then I stopped, and I was pretty good until I relapsed my second year of college."

"What happened that made you relapse?"

She squeezed her eyes shut momentarily and her face flushed for the first time. I'd never seen her ashamed before, and it made me want to hold her close.

"I was going out with this guy, and the whole relationship was so distracting that my grades suffered. When I saw my progress report, I wanted to die. We broke up pretty quickly, but it just felt like everything was unraveling, and I fell off the wagon for a week or so. Anaka, once again, was the one who helped me. I wouldn't have been able to change without her," she said softly. She stared at the jukebox, and her jaw twitched, then seemed to harden as she turned her focus back to me. "But then I got it all sorted out, and I've been fine ever since."

The last words came out too quickly, too crisply. I knew there was something more to it. Something she was afraid of sharing, but Jess wasn't prone to over-sharing, and I sensed she'd somehow reached her limit for the afternoon. I took her cue and shifted gears, too.

"You know, Jess, I'm a pretty good cook. I can make salads, and pasta with vegetables, and eggs without the yolk," I said, since I was starting to figure out she wanted someone to understand and respect her food choices, not push pizza and ice cream on her if she didn't want it.

She arched an eyebrow. "Now you're just talking dirty to me when you use words like *eggs, hold the yolk*."

There we were, back to the jokes, our familiar territory. "I knew the way to your heart was through healthy food. You're so California."

She held up a hand and shook her head. "Did I say it was the way to my heart? I believe I said *talking dirty*, which means it's the way to my"—she dropped her voice lower—"pants."

A small groan escaped my lips. I bent my head to her neck, pressing a light kiss near her earlobe, then whispered, "Lettuce. Grapefruit. Whole wheat bread."

She inhaled and moaned quietly, as if I were turning her on with my food talk. Naturally, I had to continue. Even if she was playing pretend, she was so damn sexy when her eyes floated closed and her lips parted.

"Broccoli. Carrot sticks," I said in a low, growly tone. She ran a hand across her thigh as if I were driving her wild. "Yogurt."

She turned to me, grabbed a fistful of my T-shirt, and tugged me close. "Now you're just turning me on way too much."

She might have been teasing, but I wasn't. Not one bit and I had the hard-on to prove it. This was getting to be the usual state around her. "Jess, believe me when I say there's nothing I'd rather do than turn you on," I said.

This time when her breath caught, it seemed for

real. No more pretending. "You do," she said quietly, but she quickly returned to safer ground. "Will you tail Keats and Wordsworth as well as you tailed me?"

"No. I'll do a much better job."

"You didn't do a good job tailing me?" she asked as she speared a pineapple chunk.

"I wanted to talk to you. I wanted to get to know you. I noticed you the second you walked into J.P.'s office that first day."

She held her fork in the air. She didn't bring it to her mouth. She didn't put it down. It just hovered in her hand. "From the first day?"

"Of course. You were coming through the same door."

"That's the only reason I noticed you, too. It had nothing to do with your fantastic ass," she said, then wiggled the fork with the pineapple chunk in my direction. "You know you want this pineapple, don't you?"

"Oh, I'm dying for it. Bring it here," I said, and held my mouth open. She fed me the pineapple, and I smacked my lips, declaring it delicious. I was no shrink, but I had a hunch she needed to return to her way of controlling her world, and if that was by giving me a piece of fruit, I'd let her do that. "Now, tell me more about how much you wanted me the second you laid eyes on me."

She threw her head back and laughed and it felt good to both comfort her and to make her laugh. Hell, it felt good to spend time with her. So good, in fact, that it occurred to me how much I'd miss her if the State Department sent me packing in less than two months. In a few short days, she'd somehow become one more thing I found immensely appealing about America. The thought should have scared me that I liked her this much already. But it didn't. Instead, it made me even more certain that I needed to find a way to stay.

She nodded. "So did J.P. He likes boys, too. He called you Criminally Handsome," she blurted out as if making a confession.

"I'm flattered that you checked out my ass *and* that your boss thought I was hot," I said, as I pulled my plate to her side of the table and took another bite of my sandwich.

When I finished chewing, she placed her hand on my arm, wrapping her fingers around me in a way that felt almost possessive, and I liked that from her. "Wait. Turns out, I transposed the order of events. I was the one who called you Criminally Handsome. I was the one who thought you were hot first. And I'm the one who's inviting you to come over tonight after I run some errands. You can make me a salad."

I wasn't sure if she was asking literally or if it was some new code word for dirty talk. Didn't matter. There was only one answer.

But before I could give her my yes, she continued, her eyes truthful as she caught my gaze. "And you can talk to me about salad, too."

Another groan escaped me and all I could manage was a one-word answer.

"*Yes.*"

4

Jess

This would be the scene in the movie with the shopping montage, if I were indecisive and liked to try on and model wigs. But I was decisive.

I selected a brunette model quickly from the dozen or so the sales clerk with yellowed teeth showed me. There was the long, shampoo-model look. Then the slightly wavy style. Then the housewife shoulder-length bob. Then the crazy curls. Then the boyish wig, which I vetoed because I didn't want to look like a boy at all. Finally, there was the just-long-enough-to-tuck-behind-the-ears-but-just-short-enough-to-show-off-my-neck one.

"That one," William said.

"No," I said, shaking my head.

"Why not?" he said with affront in his voice.

"It's cute, but it's just too obviously a wig. I think I have to go with slightly wavy. It's the most…" I paused, noodling on the right words. "It's the most normal. And, to be honest, the most boring. I don't want to stand out."

"Right, right," he said, refocusing on the vital mission—not getting caught on Saturday.

"May I try this on?" I asked the clerk.

"Of course. Here's a cover for your hair," the clerk said, and I took the stocking cap and the wig.

I turned to William. "You are so not seeing this part. Look the other way."

He swiveled around so he was facing the door. His back was to me. The store was tiny, with wigs on styrofoam heads stacked on shelves from floor to ceiling.

"Now, put your hands on your eyes, too."

He did as told. "Do you want to blindfold me as well?"

"I have a scarf if you want," the clerk offered. "It's behind the counter."

"Oh, please, bring it on."

"I think we'll be fine without. I'm fast." I tugged the cover over my hair, tucking my blond ponytail beneath the edge of the panty hose–like material, then pulled on the wig. I adjusted the fake hair, centering the bangless-look and tucking a strand behind my ear, to look as natural as possible.

"This one is it," I said, as I checked it out in the mirror.

"Can I look now?" he asked.

"Yes, but I'm getting this one."

I didn't wait for his reaction. I simply paid for the wig, chalking up the fifty-six dollar cost as a necessary expense for what would likely be a one hundred thousand dollar payoff.

"Can you take a picture of me in my wig?" I gestured to the white door that must have led to the back of the store. It would make a good background for a fake ID. "Is it okay to take a picture?" I asked the clerk.

"Go ahead."

I gave William my camera, and I stood against the door.

"Look mad," he teased.

I furrowed my brow.

"Perfect."

"No! Don't use that. Let's do a half smile," I said, and I knew I looked awkward because I didn't have a very good smile, but awkward would probably be appropriate for this purpose.

He took a few more shots, then showed them to me. "You approve?"

"You are a good photographer. Even though the subject is ornery."

"Didn't I tell you? My specialty is ornery subjects."

"No wonder we get along so fine," I said and put my camera away, dropping the wig in the zippered compartment, too. I slung my backpack on my shoulder, and walked out to Melrose. The sun was strong in the sky even in the early evening, and the rays felt good on my bare arms.

"We do get along fine, don't we?" he said, picking up the thread of the conversation.

"Yeah, it's weird but it's true."

Then I spotted a flash of blond hair up ahead, and the fresh-faced smile of an actress I loved. A Broadway ingénue, and my brother's wife Kat's best friend. "That's Jill McCormick," I whispered reverently to William.

"Who's she?"

"She won a Tony last year for her first ever Broadway show *Crash the Moon*. I saw her in it. My brother flew me out to New York one weekend because Jill is best friends with Kat—she was the maid of honor at my brother's wedding. We all went out after the show. Oh my God, she has the voice of an angel. And that's her husband. He was her director and they fell in love during rehearsals."

"A proper love story for that business," William said.

As Jill and Davis neared us, Jill raised her hand to wave. "Jess, is that you?"

I stopped in my tracks, as something like shock and utter delight flowed through me. "I can't believe she remembers me," I said to William.

"You're hard to forget."

Then Jill closed the gap between us and wrapped her arms around me. "How are you? So good to see you again. How's everything? Are you almost done with school?"

"Soon. I graduate in a few months," I said with a huge grin. She was so genuine. "What brings you to Los Angeles?"

She pointed her thumb at her husband, the dreamy, broody, blue-eyed Davis Milo, a legend on the Great White Way and in Hollywood, too. He'd already won an Oscar for a film he directed, along with three Tonys. "We're shooting the movie adaptation of *Crash the Moon*. Davis is directing me again."

"It seems we enjoy working together," he said, chiming in, then he extended a hand and officially introduced himself to me and to William.

We chatted more, and as we were about to say goodbye, Jill glanced down at my camera. "Are you working right now?"

"I was this afternoon," I said, because she knew I was a photographer, but I didn't want her to feel like I'd been angling for a shot.

"Want to take our picture?"

I beamed. I'd never turn down a shot. "Sure."

"Candid is better, right?" Jill asked with a wink.

"Usually, but you don't have to stage something. I can just snap a picture of the two of you."

"Oh, this won't be staged," she said, then turned to her husband, cupped his cheeks in her hands, and brushed her lips against his in a gorgeously unstaged kiss in the afternoon. They lingered on each other, and his hand skated down to her hips, as if he couldn't resist tugging her closer.

When they separated, I showed it to them on the back of the camera. "I love it," Jill said, then hugged me once more and said to keep in touch before they headed in the other direction.

"This will be great. J.P. loves a great kissing shot. Especially when they're so in love."

"They did seem to be on somewhat decent terms," William said in a dry voice.

"Yeah, just a little."

"Jess," he said as we started to walk towards our respective sets of wheels.

"Yeah?"

"I had fun with you today."

"I had fun with you, too, William."

"But I have something really important to ask about tonight."

I tensed momentarily. I had no idea what he'd want to ask or talk about. Or if he was assuming things were going in a particular direction, when I honestly wasn't sure of a thing. "What is it?"

He dropped a hand to the small of my back, then dipped his thumb under the hem of my shirt, tracing the skin on my back. "Is your roommate going to be home tonight?"

I reined in a naughty grin. "No. She has screen-writing class tonight. But that doesn't mean we're going to…" I couldn't finish.

"I know," he said, and stopped walking, pulling me against him on the sidewalk. "But even if I'm only kissing you, I'd really like to be alone with you," he said, and my stomach cartwheeled. "Would you like that?"

It was my turn now to breathe out a barely audible

yes. A single syllable constructed from hope and hormones and the wish for more with him. Then other words tumbled free. Words I'd wanted to say earlier. Words I could only say now as I started to relinquish another sliver of my carefully constructed control. "I adore kissing you."

* * *

Too bad I wasn't a makeup hound. I could have cleaned up in my mom's bathroom cabinets. Inside the white cupboard underneath the double sink was a makeup archaeologist's field day. There were eyeshadows in sky blue, electric blue, and sea green; eyeliners in black, cobalt, and chocolate brown; lipsticks in coral, rose, and scarlet; not to mention endless tubs of foundation and powder in every possible shade of skin. To top it off, the makeup here wasn't even in rotation. In her makeup suitcase—three cases tall with its own set of wheels—were the colors and cover-ups she brought with her on her jobs. I grabbed several tubs of foundation, as well as a handful of powder puffs, then left her room.

The scent of couscous emanating from the kitchen was strong and tasty. "Smells good, Mom," I called out.

"Tastes even better," she shouted in return. "You should stay."

"Can't. I have a date."

"Ooh. Tell me more."

"Ha. As if I'm going to share details of the Hot British Guy with you."

"Fine. Then just make sure you don't fall behind on homework," she said as I popped into the kitchen to give her a peck on the cheek.

"Mom, I'm ahead on homework. By the way, I told Bryan your new favorite names for twins are Bert and Ernie for boys," I said.

She narrowed her eyes and pretended to swat me with a kitchen towel.

Shrugging playfully, I egged her on. "But Kat loves those names. I'll tell her you don't and that you prefer Cagney & Lacey. That work?"

"Did you say you needed my Hollywood insider intel? Hmm. I'll have to reconsider feeding you the bits and pieces of juicy gossip I pick up," my mom said as she stirred the dish, a clever lilt in her voice.

I dropped down to my knees, ready to beg. "I'll tell them I love Chloe and Cara, too."

She nodded sagely. "You do that."

"I will. Love ya. Gotta go. Thanks for the makeup cases."

"Have fun playing spy," she said.

I crouched down to pet Jennifer on the snout before I left.

Several minutes later, as I walked up the steps to my apartment, I scrolled through my email, laughing out loud at my brother's latest picture of a dog lawyer making a joke about leashing the witness. Bryan went on to mention that the package I needed for the wedding would arrive tomorrow. I sent off a quick thanks, then clicked open the alert I'd set up for the Bowman-Belle wedding. There was a short item in *On the Surface*.

As the two-day countdown until the fabled Bowman-Belle wedding begins, a well-placed source at a party rental store confirms to *On the Surface* that an order for a tent large enough for two hundred guests, along with folding white chairs and a white runner, is being prepared for a Saturday morning delivery to a well-known Hollywood residence in Malibu.

I smiled as I read the item. Flash worked for *On the Surface*. She'd probably be scouting this well-known residence in Malibu all day Saturday, along with the rest of my paparazzi brethren. But they didn't know where the wedding really was. Let them all run around Malibu empty-handed.

Inside the apartment, Anaka was gathering her materials for class, scooping up papers from the table. They'd been tucked under a makeshift paperweight— her coconut hand lotion.

She stopped to say hi. "Hey! I have the purse you asked for for the wedding. Hold on."

She scurried to her room and returned with a light-beige purse. I inspected the inside of the tan shoulder bag.

"Perfect. Let's see how it looks," she said.

I draped it on my shoulder. It fell to my ribs, which was the perfect length. I didn't want a purse that dangled against my hip. I needed one that I could keep a tight grip on.

"Looks awesome," she said, darting into the kitchen to grab a pair of long-handled scissors. She handed them to me, then shielded her eyes. "Just don't deface it till I leave."

"Your purse had a good life," I said solemnly.

She pretended to sob as she zipped up her messenger bag for class. "The purse is willing to lay down its life in the service of duty. Besides, you fed Karina the Rain photo and I've been watching my blog traffic go way up tonight. Karina's people love pictures of Rain and his silly little vests."

"Speaking of photos, I still haven't seen one turn up yet of the pictures I took of Riley the night before."

"I bet they're waiting to run them in the morning or something. The best time for a site is always in the morning. The only reason I post my entries at night is I lack something known as patience."

My phone rang, and I looked at the screen on my phone. "Says *private*."

Anaka squealed. "That means it's Riley. Answer it and tell me everything later. I need to run."

"Doubtful," I said as she walked out the door, and I answered the call.

"Hello?"

"Hi, I'm looking for Jess, and I can't believe I never got your last name."

Anaka's radar was 100 percent accurate. I'd recognize Riley Belle's voice anywhere. I'd seen all her movies.

"Hey. This is Jess. Jess Leighton," I added.

"It's Riley Belle. And you can't see him, but little Mr. Sparky McDoodle is here with me in my lap. He says hello. He says thank you again. He says *I love you*," she said, and then laughed, her laughter sounding like the tinkle of a pretty church bell.

"How is Mr. Sparky McDoodle? All good, I assume?"

"He's perfect. I bought him a new sweater last night after the incident. He was so rattled, and he always settles down when he has new clothes," she said, then laughed. "I'm just kidding. He's not that kind of dog. He doesn't care about clothes."

I laughed, too, though I felt uneven. I wasn't sure how to behave with her. She wasn't what I had pictured. She liked to poke fun at herself. It was strangely refreshing, even as it was unexpected.

"So, Jess. I totally want to take you out, like I promised. I have to tell you that I can't stop thinking about what you did for my dog yesterday, and I am so grateful. There's this amazing place along the beach," she said, and then named the hottest new eatery in town, and I didn't bother to ask how we'd get in when it was well known the waiting list was months—long after being declared the best brunch on the West Coast in a fancy food magazine. We'd get in because she was Riley Belle.

"It sounds awesome." Obviously, I wasn't going to say no. "When?"

"Let's see. Tomorrow's Friday, and my lawyer's in town from New York, so we're meeting in the morning to review possible projects for my production company. You have no idea how hard it is to find a good script these days," she said, and she reminded me of my chat with Anaka kvetching about the same problem last night. "And speaking of problems with scripts, then I'm going to be at the studio in the afternoon for a final read-through of *The Weekenders* because the director made *another* last-minute change to the script after last night's run-through." I cringed a bit inside when she mentioned last night, because twenty-four hours ago I was snapping her face lip-locked with Avery Brock and figuring she'd never call, so I'd never have to feel guilty. Now she'd called, and now I felt mighty guilty. "But that's neither here nor there, so Friday's a no-go. And Saturday is out because I have this wedding thing to be at on Saturday and it's going to last all night."

"Right. Your sister's getting married. You must be so excited," I said, then wanted to kick myself. I sounded like a starstruck sycophant.

"I'm so excited for her, too. I'm going to be a bridesmaid, and it's going to be amazing. I guess we should make it a Sunday brunch, since I have a thing on Sunday night."

A thing probably meant a second tryst with Avery Brock.

"Let me just check my calendar and see if I'm free on Sunday," I said in a playful voice, pretending to thumb through a calendar. I needed to recover and return to the funny girl Riley thought I was yesterday.

Because that's the girl I wanted to be, not a yes woman. "Okay, turns out I'm available."

She laughed briefly. "Perfect. Can we do eleven? Is that too late? I'm just worried about getting to the restaurant on time after Saturday's festivities."

"Not a problem. I'll see you and Sparky McDoodle at eleven on Sunday."

"Yay. Can't wait, Jess."

The call ended, and I studied the phone as if it would emit a report verifying that I really did have a phone conversation with Riley Belle. Was I becoming friends with an actress? It was an odd notion, but then I was becoming friends, too, with a private detective who'd been following me, and now was my partner-in-sort-of-crime as well as my oh-so-hot-date in an hour, so odd notions were not unfamiliar this week.

I flopped down on my bed, resting my head on my pillow, flashing back to today in the diner, and in the wig shop, and on the street with William. We'd had fun, I'd felt carefree with him, as if I didn't have the weight of the world on my shoulders. I'd even confessed something I rarely told anyone. But I wanted him to know the real me, not just the me I presented.

Why did I want him to know me?

Because I liked him. I more than liked him. I also liked who I could be with him. With him I wasn't merely the Jess who wanted to be a doctor, who earned top grades, who kept all her emotions in check. That Jess was restrained. She always had the proper handle on any situation.

But there was another Jess, the one who planned disguises, the one who was daring enough to chase down pictures, the one who let insults and invectives from stars who didn't want their photos taken slide off her.

The one I was with him.

5

William

I had an address for tomorrow, some Web research for tonight, and a shopping bag full of the ingredients for chicken stir-fry.

The one item I didn't have? Time to tail the boy poets. I had yet to bend the time-space continuum of Los Angeles traffic far enough to track the brothers in the three hours I had free in between saying goodbye to Jess and knocking on the door of her apartment. But I was armed with *other* information, and intel was yet another way to her heart, so I'd take that route for now. I wanted to win her over.

More of her.

When she opened the door, my eyes nearly popped out of my head. Words rattled around in my brain but I could barely gather them in a coherent fashion.

"Skirt," I mumbled, as proper construction of sentences and little details like verbs fled my mind. I was unable to take my eyes off her legs. Her strong, toned, bare legs were on display for the first time. I'd only ever seen her in jeans, and now she was wearing a jean skirt that hit her mid-thigh—God bless short skirts—and a light blue tank top. Her blond hair was swept up in a ponytail that showed off her neck and shoulders. But the skirt, that was all I could think of… well, all I could think of was what was underneath the skirt. How her thighs would feel in my hands. How soft her skin might be.

"Skirt," she said, making a rolling gesture with her hands as if she was supplying me with the missing word.

I shook my head, like a dog shaking off water. "You're wearing a skirt," I said. My jaw was possibly still scraping the floor.

"Very good, William. You have excellent sartorial identification skills." She gestured to me. "You're wearing jeans and a T-shirt," she said, as if speaking to a young child. "Now, can you try naming this?" She tugged on the fabric of her tank top.

Recovering the power of speech and the use of brain cells, I stepped inside, shut the door, and set my bag down on the floor. I reached for the shirt, taking the fabric in my hand as I pulled her in close, brushed my lips along her neck, and whispered in her ear. "Something I want to take off."

She breathed in sharply, and shivered against me. "Tables turned," she said in a low, sexy purr.

I nibbled on her earlobe then dropped my mouth to her lips, covering her in a kiss that I had no choice but to give. Kissing her was not optional. It was mandatory, and as necessary as air or breath. She tilted her face to me, and I deepened the kiss, my tongue meeting hers, tasting, licking, and touching her with the kind of recklessness that some kisses demand. That's how I felt—beholden to this kiss as her apartment faded away, as the music from her iPod drifted out the window, because all my senses narrowed to the press of her lips against mine.

Eventually, we came up for air.

"So, I brought bell peppers, chicken, and the most fantastic dessert," I said quickly, segueing playfully into dinner as if that kiss hadn't just nailed me right in the heart.

She ran a hand through her bangs, as if she was clearing her head. "Sounds perfect."

She showed me to the kitchen and I told her I had good news.

"You already started tailing the brothers?" she asked, her eyes lighting up.

I laughed and roped my arms around her waist, kissing her hair as I moved behind her to start emptying the shopping bag. "I know the way to your heart. Rabbit food and clues."

"I'm easy like that. So tell me stuff," she said, handing me a skillet, spray oil, a knife, and a cutting board.

"I did some prelim research online. I found where Keats and Wordsworth live, so I'm going to scope them out tomorrow. I also tracked down one vital piece of information already. You know that website for Keats's agency?"

"Yes."

"He registered the domain name about three days ago. The site just went up this week, Jess."

She shivered as if a chill ran through her. "So…"

"I don't know what to make of it yet, but I think it's safe to say he's probably not a legit agency," I said as I began chopping peppers.

"Crap," she said, blowing a frustrated stream of air through her lips. "I should have looked into that. I never thought to look into it."

"Of course not. It all seemed real. He seemed real," I said, as I pushed the orange bell peppers to the side of the cutting board, moving on to the yellow ones. "The money was real, and he paid you in cash. You're not the one he's setting up. As much as it might seem like he's setting you up, I don't think you're who he's trying to frame."

"Who are Keats and Wordsworth setting up, then? Riley? That would make me feel so guilty," she said, dropping her forehead into her palm. "Riley was sweet, and she was happy, and she seemed genuinely eager to have brunch."

"I don't know. But listen, I only have one class tomorrow, so I'll be out bright and early and I'll follow them and see if I can figure out something."

As I set aside the chopped peppers and began working on carrots and broccoli, she nodded. "Okay. But I think you should follow Jenner. If they were both having lunch with Jenner, he's probably the one setting her up."

"That's what I was thinking, too. See, great minds think alike," I said, then scooped up the peppers, carrots, and broccoli onto a separate plate before I tackled sautéing the pre-cut cubes of diced chicken.

We chatted for a bit more about the threesome of sneaky Hollywood players as I cooked.

She lifted her nose in the air and sniffed. "Smells yummy."

"Why, thank you. I hope you love it," I said, choosing for once not to make a joke. I truly did want her to be happy with what I served. Not only because food was challenging for her, but because I wanted to impress her. I wanted to impress her in the kitchen, with my conversation, and with my hands, lips, and tongue. As well as other instruments.

"What were you doing before I came over?" I asked, as I finished the dish and turned down the heat on the stove. "Doing curls or crunches or studying for your first bio exam next fall, right? Wait, you were making a spreadsheet of celebrity sightings and likelihood of whereabouts."

She smiled brightly at me. "You think I'm hyper prepared?" she asked, but she wasn't bothered that I'd figured out that she was.

"Well, you do have flash cards, don't you?"

"That reminds me—I need to add publicists' faces to my cards."

"Oh, well, don't let me keep you," I said as I began plating the food.

"It's okay. I can do it when you leave," she said with a sexy little wink, as if it was some naughty secret that she was a workaholic.

"What if I keep you busy all night, though?" I asked as I ran a hand along the waistband of her skirt on my way to the table.

"You've got a lot of stamina, then," she replied.

"I do, Jess. I absolutely do."

"Maybe I'll find out how much someday," she said, lowering her voice to a flirty whisper, the words heating me up.

"Maybe you will. For now, this is your one and only chance to eat this fantastic dinner because after that I'm going to have a hard time keeping my hands off of you."

She opened her fridge, waggled a beer bottle at me in offering, raising her eyebrows to ask if I wanted it.

"Of course."

Then she took one for herself, which surprised me, but made me happy, too, because it meant she wasn't depriving herself of something worth having due to calories. Even though she only drank one-quarter of it while we ate dinner.

6

Jess

The pans were washed, the dishes were dried, and the meal was officially delicious. The conversation was great, too. William and I had talked the whole time at dinner—I told him more about my favorite movies and how I got into photography, and I even told him about the pictures I still felt guilty about. The ones I took of Nick Ballast.

He shook his head. "Don't feel guilty, Jess. It shows you're a good person that you feel that way, but truly, everyone is responsible for what they do and their own choices. Just like you. You've taken control of things, and you live your life the way you want now, and Nick is doing the same."

"Thank you for saying that," I said, and hearing

that from him made another small layer of guilt shear off.

Then it was his turn to share, and he told me about the summer he spent in Italy learning the language, and about how frustrated he felt at times for not having a job yet.

"It's like I keep trying with James, and in all these other places, too, and it's not happening yet. It makes me feel like I'm not good enough," he admitted in a quiet voice as we put the final dishes away.

William was usually so confident, so sure of himself. But the frustration in his tone was tangible and I would have felt it, too, in his situation.

"You are good enough," I said firmly. "You just haven't met the right job yet."

That made him laugh. "Like when you say to your unmarried spinster aunt, *you haven't met the right guy yet?*"

"Exactly. But I believe it. There's a job for you. You just have to keep looking. And besides, it seems like you're good at everything. Let me get this straight. You speak twenty languages, ride a bike, have a six-pack, a hot accent, *and* you can cook?" I arched an eyebrow.

"Oh please. You're embarrassing me," he said, holding up his hands in mock humility, as we settled down on the couch. He lowered his voice to a stage whisper. "I only speak five languages."

"Somewhere, there are a bunch of guys who got the short end of the stick. They're sitting around at some sorry dudes meeting, moping about how there was a completely uneven distribution of assets when you were born," I said, and William simply smiled at the compliment.

"See? That's another thing. Great smile. It's like you took everything and left the rest of the guys with nothing," I said as I reached for the dessert bowl on the table that was filled with blueberries. I popped one into my mouth.

"My, my. Haven't you taken a one-eighty," he said, scooping a handful of blueberries for himself.

"Or maybe I'm just being nice to you because you're following those guys for me," I said, returning to our familiar way of teasing. In a flash, he dropped the blueberries from his hand into the bowl, grabbed my wrists, and pinned me. Flat on my back on the couch, my breath came fast as he hovered over me.

"Take it back," he said, his dark gray eyes locked on mine. "Take it back or I'll have no choice but to show you why you like having me around," he said darkly, pressing his groin against me in demonstration.

My skin heated in an instant. I was sure I was burning up all over. "Show me," I whispered, daring him on. He wedged a strong leg between my thighs, spreading my legs open. He lowered himself to me, grinding his pelvis against me in the most excruciatingly slow tease. My brain cells decamped, and rational thought fled the building. Here, on my couch, with music playing faintly in the background, the sounds of Los Angeles evening traffic from the nearby avenue filtering through the open windows, all I wanted was him. He hadn't even kissed me, and I was desperate for more.

"Take it back," he said again, his voice a hot whisper on my neck. My eyes fluttered closed with the scratch of his stubble against me, and the slow grind of his hard-on against the fabric of my jean skirt. I willed him to push it up, to gather my skirt at my waist and tug down my panties, but that was the hormones talking. I knew I wasn't ready to be naked with him.

Yet.

But even as lust clouded my brain, I managed to speak. "I'm just teasing. I like you, William," I said, laying out the truth. I opened my eyes and looked into his, and they were filled with satisfaction, but happiness, too. "You know that, right?"

"I know. I just like hearing it," he admitted.

"And I'm really glad you're following them. Not only because I want to know what they're up to but because I like that we're working together," I said, looking up at him. I was still pinned, my arms above my head, my wrists in his hands, and I loved every second of this position.

"Me, too," he said softly.

"I feel like we're partners, and it means a lot to me that you're doing this and helping. I know you're trying to get a job with your uncle's firm, so the fact that you're doing all this for me means so much."

"I want to help, Jess. I want to help *you*," he said, his voice sweet as he spoke in a bare whisper. Gone were our usual playful barbs and snark; in their place was only honesty and vulnerability. Those twin emotions scared the hell out of me, but they also felt good. I wasn't accustomed to being vulnerable and letting down my guard, but I'd come to trust William. And I was starting to see—or to *feel*—the benefits of letting him in. This afternoon at the diner, he'd been so caring. Like he was now, too.

Which made me realize that was yet another trait he had in the positive column.

"I like it when you help me," I whispered, and he let go of my wrists to bury his hands in my hair and kiss me. It was a tender kiss, one that made me tremble as he swept his tongue across my lips, taking his time before he deepened the kiss, all while running the pad of his thumb along my jawline. There was something so gentle, but possessive, too, about the way he touched my face as he kissed me. My heart leapt in my chest, like it was trying to get closer to him.

As soon as that thought touched down in my head, I tensed. Because I was falling for him. Big time. I had no clue what liking him this much would do to me. To my control. To my studies. To my quest to stay healthy. To my future. Especially when his future was so uncertain. I stopped the kiss. He pulled back.

"Are you okay?" he asked, brushing my hair away from my cheek.

"Yes," I said, then swallowed. I pressed my lips together so I wouldn't speak, wouldn't reveal all that I was starting to feel.

"Are you sure?"

I nodded.

"You don't look okay," he said, moving off me to lie next to me. "What happened? I think you kind of checked out. I'm a terrible kisser, right?" he said, flashing me that trademark grin that melted me all the way to the ends of my hair and the tips of my toes. That feeling—like happiness flooding through my veins—was enough to make me talk. I didn't want to lose this sensation, even for a moment. It was a feeling that wasn't borne from doing well in school or nabbing a photo or checking off another item on my to-do list. It was from falling.

"You know I love kissing you. I was just thinking about what happens when…" I let my voice trail off.

He picked up the thread easily. "When I might have to go back to England?"

"Yes."

"Me, too," he said in a soft voice, as if the question weighed on him.

"I mean, I like you. But what can this even be? It's so hard to find a job."

"I know," he sighed heavily. "Trust me. I know."

"Do you even think you'll stay?"

"I want to. So much. And I like you. So much," he said, and stopped to look at me, his eyes hooking into me. "And maybe now you're yet another reason I really want to stay."

My eyes widened, and I felt the breath knocked out of me. "I am?"

He bent his head to my neck, pressing a soft kiss against my skin before he looked back into my eyes. "Yes. Does that scare you?"

I shrugged. "A little. I mean we only met three days ago."

"I know," he said, running his hand along my hip.

"And I have no clue what's going to happen. All I know is I enjoy hanging out with you immensely, and I want more of you."

A ribbon of worry cut through me. *More of me.* Did I have any more to give? I was stretched thin with work, and school, and volunteering, let alone going to medical school next fall. How on earth could I ever give any more of myself? But yet, I couldn't deny that being with William was the one pure spot of pleasure in my life. He was chocolate, he was cake, he was ice cream, and I wanted to gobble him up. The moments with him were the times when I wasn't wound tight. I could let go with him. I wouldn't be able to let go at all next year, or for the next four years once medical school started. Maybe more of him was exactly what I needed right now. A finite amount of more. Not a commitment. Not a promise. Just a smidgeon. He gently took hold of my hand, threading his fingers through mine.

"I want that, too, but getting close worries me," I admit. "I don't want to relapse or anything."

"I completely respect that. I truly do, but you're stronger than you think, Jess. I know you worry that you have to have the world rotating at the perfect pace and everything going a certain way. But if anyone has it together, Jess, it's you."

I didn't answer right away. Instead, I soaked up his words and the way he seemed to know me so well already. Maybe I could have it all. Maybe I was stronger than I thought when it came to guys and food. Maybe I was on the other side of my eating disorder.

"And look," he continued. "I don't know if I'm staying or going. I have no clue what happens. All I know is the last few days with you have been fantastic and I would love to keep seeing you while I'm here. I would love it if you'd be my girlfriend."

Girlfriend. It was as if all the sound zipped out of the apartment at once, turning the air silent. I hadn't been anyone's girlfriend in a long time, and my body froze at the prospect. But then I thawed because being with him was safe. I wouldn't let myself get too close with him possibly leaving, and with me starting school next fall. Maybe I could truly have my cake and eat it, too.

Him.

"You're kind of like cake," I murmured.

He raised an eyebrow in question.

"You're like cake to me and I want cake," I added.

He laughed, a deep, rumbly belly laugh that seemed to echo in the room, filling it back up with noise and the sweetness of laughter. "Knowing how you feel about food, I will happily be your cake."

"Then come back on top of me because that felt pretty good, what you were doing earlier," I said, and in a heartbeat he was over me again, his hard body aligning with mine.

"Hi," he whispered.

"Hi," I said back, and something about this moment felt like we had stepped over a line and onto the other side.

He rocked against me, his erection pressed hard into my thigh. I shivered as a wave of goosebumps rushed over my skin. I closed my eyes and leaned my head back, giving in to the letting go.

"I love touching you, Jess. For so many reasons," he said as he rubbed against me. "But especially because I like watching you let go of your grip on the world."

"You do?"

"Yes," he said, thrusting against me. "I do. I love it. I love how it's the one time when you let yourself feel good. I love that you do that with me."

"You make me feel good," I said, my breath feathering against his cheek.

"I would love to make you feel even better," he said, and a flurry of white-hot sparks ignited in my belly with the suggestion. Heat pooled between my legs, and I was dying for him to touch me.

"How?" I asked as I looped my hands around to his ass, dipping them back into his jeans once more.

"However you'll let me," he said, his voice turning low and husky and so full of need. He wanted me to feel good, wanted me to let go beneath him, and that sounded pretty damn appealing to me, too. Better than cake, better than chocolate. Touching him was like having all the things I kept at a distance.

"What you're doing right now feels pretty fantastic," I said as we rocked together, my hips arching into his erection. "But maybe just take off my skirt," I whispered.

In seconds, he'd unbuttoned, unzipped, and

tugged off my skirt. I lay before him on the couch, wearing only my tank top and a simple pair of cotton boy shorts in dark blue that hugged me low on my hips.

"Fuck," he hissed out as he looked at me, and I couldn't help but thrill at his reaction. His raw, unedited reaction to seeing my panties. Such a simple moment, but such an intimate one, too. "My favorite color on you," he rasped out as he ran his fingers against the cotton panel of my panties, feeling where I was wet for him. "You're so hot," he said. "I love that I did this to you."

"You did. Now do more," I instructed as I grabbed him by the hips and yanked him down against me. I wasn't ready for his hands in my pants, or his mouth. But the feel of him against me? That I could manage, and that's what he gave me as he began grinding against me.

I moaned with every move he made, arching my back, and gripping his butt hard as he rocked perfectly into me. So damn perfectly that I could feel that delicious start of something. The slow, sweet spread of pleasure all throughout my body. The sensation that a decadent release was within my reach.

"*William*," I moaned, rocking into him, as waves began to crest inside me.

He said something in Italian. I had no clue what he was saying, but it sounded dirty, and I loved the possibility of the words. He rained kisses on my bare skin, brushing his lips against my throat, my neck, my ear as he moved his body against mine in a dizzying pace, his hard length doing wonders to me even through the layers between us. It didn't matter that our clothes were on, it didn't matter that his skin wasn't touching mine. I was close, so close, and nothing was going to stop this orgasm that hovered on the edge of my evening with him.

"Oh God," I gasped, opening my legs wider and wrapping them around his hips. "It feels so good," I moaned.

"I want you to feel amazing."

And I did feel amazing. Absolutely out of this world incredible as I started seeing stars, bright and beautiful, like the way I felt when I was with him. I wrapped my arms tighter around him, pulled him as close as he could possibly be, and my mouth fell open into an O as my body went there, too.

William

So. Yeah. That was hot. Like, crazy hot. I was dying to slide my hand inside her panties, to feel how wet she was, to have her rock against my fingers. But all I really wanted was for Jess to feel good, and for me to be the one to make her feel that way. For her to come just from the friction of our bodies made me want to pound my chest.

But I wasn't that type of guy. Instead, I kissed her more because I couldn't resist. Her lips were delicious, her skin was divine, and her body melted whenever I touched her. Nothing was a bigger turn-on than when the girl you like loses control as you touch her. Jess was like that with me, and the way we connected in the bedroom—okay, living room—was yet another reason I wanted more and more of her.

"That was so fucking hot," I said after I broke the kiss.

A faint smile curved her lips, and she still wore the afterglow of an orgasm on her face—flushed cheeks, plump red lips, and eyes hazy with desire fulfilled. "It was so fucking hot," she repeated, and I loved that she wasn't embarrassed or shy from coming while I—let's call a spade a spade, shall we? —dry humped her.

She roped her arms around my neck and pulled me back in for more kisses, looping her legs tight around me again. Maybe she was ready for another, and hell, I was up to the task. Very, very up to it.

"You liked my legs, didn't you?" she asked.

"Hmmm?" Her question didn't compute.

Then in seconds, she gripped me with her thighs and flipped me with those strong legs. I was on my back, and she was wedged along the couch by my side. Her hands were fast, and she moved quickly, unzipping my jeans and grasping my hard-on through my boxer briefs.

I groaned loudly, my eyes floating closed as she touched me. She felt so incredibly good, her quick hand rubbing me. I was reduced to nothing but the desire for her to touch me more. Fortunately, she didn't need me to tell her that. She knew, because she tugged at my jeans, then my boxers, pulling them down far enough to take me in her hand.

Holy fuck. Her soft fingers wrapped around me, and all the air escaped my lungs as she stroked me. "Your hands are like magic," I rasped out as I rocked into her palm.

"They'll feel even better like this," she said, breaking the contact for a second. I opened my eyes to watch her lean across me and grab a bottle of lotion from the coffee table, and pump some into her hand.

"Always thinking," I said, wiggling my eyebrows.

"Lubrication works wonders," she said, returning to my erection and gripping me harder.

"That it does, Jess. That it—" I stopped talking when she started using both hands, stroking and tugging in ways that made my whole body vibrate. I sank down into the couch, giving in to the moment with her, to the way her talented hands worked me over.

"God, I want to fuck you so badly," I said to her in Italian.

"I have no clue what you're saying, but I bet it's dirty," she said, laughing as she grasped me in such perfect harmony, using both hands. Sheer pleasure ricocheted throughout my bones and blood as she pumped her hands over me, on me, against me.

"So fucking dirty. I am dying to be inside you, to feel you come on me, to have you under me," I said in that language, too, another groan working its way up my throat as her hands flew faster, the lotion doing its job of turning friction into wonderful abandon.

"I love that you talk in Italian when you get turned on," she said, and this time it was her voice, her hands, the fresh memory of the sexy way she'd arched against me, that set me off into a fantastic climax.

I bit off a string of endless curse words as I thrust hard into her hand.

Minutes later, when we'd both cleaned up, I wrapped an arm around her and pulled her in close. "See, and that's another reason why I hope I can stay in America. All that cake."

She tensed for the briefest of seconds, then relaxed into me.

I had no idea if she wanted the same things I did —more—but for now I had her, so I'd take what I could get.

FRIDAY

FRIDAY

Weather: 70 degrees, Sunny

7

Jess

I stretched out my hamstrings at the foot of the trail as I listened to my most upbeat pre-running playlist. There was nothing quite like a jog on the trails as the sun rose. Plus, I was even more energetic than usual. Having a fantastic orgasm last night delivered by a hot guy I was crazy for *might* have had something to do with the good mood that fueled my morning. He'd already texted me at the crack of dawn. His message had sent flurries down my spine.

HBG: Hi. I think I'm still high this morning on you. Can we have a repeat tonight?

I'd said yes, of course. That man had worked his way into my heart, and somehow he had the secret key to unlock my body. Because the simplest touch from him turned me all the way on. Even his notes unleashed goosebumps in me.

Another note arrived as I moved on to calf stretches.

HBG: Will start the tail soon. Uncle James has demanded I appear at his office this morning. Says he needs to review wedding plans, so at least my delay is for a good cause.

I wrote back: *A very good cause.*

While bouncing on my toes, my phone rattled in my hand once more. Sliding my finger over the screen, I expected another text from William but instead opened a message from my dad.

Guess who's history from The Weekenders?? Nick Ballast. Otherwise known as Nick Balloons!

My Hollywood-gossip-loving eyes widened to full saucer size as I read his note, and the way he'd used the tabloid moniker my shots had inspired for the once tubby Nick. I tapped out a quick reply.

Nick's been cut from The Weekenders? Did the studio boot him?

Ever the early bird, my dad replied quickly.

The director nixed him. Your mom heard about it this morning from a friend who's an agent at WAM, since a WAM client has been recast in Nick's role.

I gulped, a new fear swooping through me as I dialed my dad—the possibility that I was to blame. "Already? The studio already recast the part?" I asked, quickly segueing from text to talking.

"Crazy, isn't it? That movie's a mess. The script languishes in rewrite hell for the better part of the decade, then more rewrites before shooting, then a cast member axed a week or so before it starts production."

"But who replaced him, Dad?" I asked, as a cold dread seeped through me. I feared I knew who he'd say.

"Jenner Davies. Of all people, Jenner Davies."

I stumbled back, and grabbed hold of a fencepost at the head of the trail.

"You okay?"

"Yeah. I guess his charitable makeover campaign worked even better than he planned," I said heavily. But it wasn't his makeover campaign that had won him a part. It was blackmail.

"That's why the photos of Riley and Avery never ran," I said to Anaka, frustration laced through my voice as the sun began its trek up the sky, casting early morning light across the hills. "They were never designed to run. They were taken for leverage, and Jenner used that leverage to blackmail Avery Brock into dumping Nick and stealing the role of the sixth student in weekend detention. Avery didn't want his indiscretions to get out."

All because of me. Because I was seduced by money. Because I hadn't thought to do the simplest of background checks on Keats Wharton. I'd believed he was who he said he was.

"Don't berate yourself, sweetie." Anaka said after I

told her everything as I hiked. I was too upset to jog, so I was power walking, and talking.

"But it's my fault he lost the part, Anaka."

"How would you have possibly known this would happen?" she said, then yawned deeply. I'd woken her up. She liked to sleep in on Fridays, but I wasn't ready to call William this morning and discuss it with him. I needed to talk this out with my closest friend.

"I don't know. But I should have been smarter. I mean, how many one-year-out-of-college-graduates run photo agencies?"

"How many college students earn a part-time living as a paparazzo? Only one," she countered. "You."

"Two, actually. There's another girl, but I think she's nineteen," I said, thinking of Flash.

"Fine. One, two, whatever. It's practically the same, and my point is he seemed totally plausible, and he paid you in cash."

I stopped walking, and pressed my thumb and forefinger hard against the bridge of my nose. "I just feel so stupid," I said in a low voice, as I moved to the side of the trail to let a headphone-wearing guy run past me.

"But, Jess. There's no way you could have known Jenner was behind it."

"If I had studied up on publicists in Hollywood, I might have."

"Beat yourself up some more. It's so good for you. But even if you studied the faces of every publicist in

LA, you wouldn't necessarily have been able to pick out the younger brother of Jenner Davies's publicist. That's why Jenner and the other dude sent the younger brother. To fool you. They planned it all out. They plotted it. And you have to admit, they did a damn good job."

I resumed my walk, and breathed out hard. "Yeah, they did," I said. From the website, to the other photo placements, to the business cards, the plan was beyond solid, and I might never have even known about the ruse if I hadn't stumbled upon the three of them toasting at Rosanna's Hideout when I went to retrieve my toothpaste. Keats had played me all right, but I was merely an unimportant pawn. The real chess piece was Jenner Davies checkmating Avery Brock.

The teen actor with the angry attitude had found his way back on screen with a bribe. And Avery Brock was exactly the type of person who was susceptible to blackmail, because blackmail only works when you have something to hide. Avery had a lot to cover up. It was ironic how I'd thought Riley was being set up by the poet brothers, when Avery turned out to be the real target. But where there was a target, there was a victim. That victim was Nick, and he was the innocent bystander with the wound from the bullet he didn't see coming. I couldn't just let him take the hit and lose a job. I had to make good for him.

"I'm going to call Keats and confront him," I announced to Anaka, feeling like I was taking charge of the situation.

"What good will that do?"

"I don't know. But I feel bad for what happened to Nick. Given our, you know…"

"Your history," she said, finishing the sentence. "As photographer and subject, Jess."

"Yeah, and now my photos of someone else have hurt him again," I said, guilt pinging through my chest.

"Look, I hate to say this, but you're one of the winners here."

I scoffed. "Winners? How do you figure?"

"You got paid. You got paid well. You made out okay," Anaka said, talking coolly and calmly through the situation. "Look, Jenner had something on Avery Brock. He knew Avery was up to something, and so he sensed an opportunity and he took advantage of it. That's what Hollywood is. That's what Hollywood does. You should know as well as anyone. You document this stuff all the time, and the only reason it *seems* different now is you feel like you know the people. But this affair was going to happen. And someone was going to get the shots. And someone was going to use them to his advantage, whether or not you were involved."

She was right. There was an inevitability to the whole ruse. If Keats hadn't found me, he would have tracked down another photographer. Still, this was one of those times when I felt about myself the way a lot of other people did about the paparazzi.

That we were scum.

I hung up with Anaka, blocked my number, and called Keats, hoping I'd catch him off guard. There was just something about a call from a private number that made Los Angelenos pick up their phones.

"Keats here," he said, and I wanted to smack him. He was playing the part and talking like a business-man, even though he was an actor like everyone else.

"I wanted to commend you for your perfor-mance," I said as I climbed up a series of switchbacks on the trail.

"Excuse me? Who's this?"

"Just the 'girl after your own heart,' remember?" I said, quoting himself back to him.

"Oh, Jess. Good morning."

"Not such a good morning for Nick Ballast, though, is it? I know what you and your brother did. I know who your brother is. Jenner's publicist. I know you guys have something on Avery, and so your brother and Jenner blackmailed Avery to get on the movie."

"Whoa. You're making a lot of assumptions."

"But none of them are wrong. So they're not really assumptions. It's kind of scummy, don't you think?"

He laughed so hard it was as if he was barking through the phone line. "You take pictures of actors and directors cheating with each other and I'm scum?"

When he said that, I smiled, because I remem-bered I had a trump card. The person who takes the pictures almost always does. I wasn't going to play it yet, but play it I would. "But the point is someone got hurt here. Nick Ballast had nothing to do with any of this. With you, with Jenner, or with Avery. And now he lost his job because of what you guys did. That's just wrong."

"Nick Ballast is a big boy. I have a feeling he'll be just fine."

"You can't know that. Besides, Jenner's plan won't work if everyone knows what's going on, right?" I asked, showing the corner of that trump card. Let him squirm.

I could hear Keats rustling around, maybe getting out of bed, standing up, starting to worry. "What do you mean?"

"Jenner's leverage was that he'd keep Avery's affair a secret in exchange for the role in *The Weekenders*, right? If everyone knew Avery was fooling around with Riley, Jenner would have no leverage to get the part in the first place," I said, even as I wondered how Jenner had known that Avery and Riley were hooking up. How would Jenner have been privy to that info? "But if the pictures got out…"

"You're not going to share the pictures, Jess," Keats said, but his voice wavered. He didn't know what I'd do. He didn't know me.

"I have the copies. I have the files. I could get them to any photo agency and onto any site in seconds."

"But you won't," Keats said, and now his voice was firm and commanding. I slowed my pace. "Because I anticipated this might happen. And that's why my brother and I picked you. Not because of your shots of Riley and Miles. Because you're putting yourself through college, and then medical school by taking pictures. We researched you, Jess. We did our homework," he said, and a chill ran down my spine. "Call me crazy, but I don't think J.P. and whatever agencies you work for would be happy when they hear you backstab your clients. Because I'm your client, Jess. Whether you like it or not. You deposited the money. You were paid. You want all the photo agencies in town to know you take their money and then turn around and threaten them?"

Silence gripped my throat, like a hand clamping down. I seared inside from the hot shame of his threat. And from the harsh truth of his statement. I wanted to punch him. Not only because he was hitting below the belt, but because he'd found my weak spot, and was using it against me. My Achilles' heel. My dreams, my hope, my future of medical school and the way I paid for it—the way I *had* to pay for it. I felt like Avery Brock. I felt like that dick of a director because Keats had leverage on me now.

He was right. I couldn't turn on him because then I'd be known for doing just that. I'd never work in this town again.

"You go ahead and run those pictures and I'll make sure every photo agency knows how you do business."

"You're an ass," I said through gritted teeth.

"Yeah. Probably. That's why I'll be good in this business. It's cutthroat."

"And what are you going to do when other photogs take pictures of Avery? You know someone else will catch him on camera with Riley. It's the inevitable law of Hollywood hooking up," I said, scrambling to regain some kind of foothold.

"The deal will be done by then. The movie will have started shooting with Jenner in the role. We moved first, and we moved fast, and that's what matters. Avery won't replace another actor."

"You don't know that," I pointed out.

"I'll take my chances. But look, it was nice doing business with you. And hey, my hat's off to you. You played it well. You thought you had me. But in the end, Jess, we both get to walk away having gotten what we wanted. I guess you are a girl after my own black and twisted heart. We're just a couple of players in Hollywood after all. Here's to dealmaking."

He hung up first, and I stared at the phone, my head pounding with the anger of having been played. I pushed my hair out of my face, blowing a frustrated sigh across my lips.

"Heads up."

I turned around in time to press myself against a tree to let a group of pink shorts–wearing middle-aged women run past me. They must be a running group, training for a breast cancer run together, because they were led by a younger woman, who was cheering them on and shouting motivational phrases.

A personal trainer.

As I let them pass, I flashed back on the image of Nick Ballast and his trainer from earlier in the week, recalling that they ran not far from here. Excitement flared in me, the daring possibility that I could make things right. That I could fix my mistake by telling the one person who could do something about this whole mess I'd made.

Nick.

Because this was my real trump card—not photos, but encyclopedic knowledge of celebrities' where-abouts. I knew where stars hung out. I had studied them, memorized their routines, and committed their every habit to memory.

Turning around, I ran as fast as I could back to my scooter. I yanked on my helmet and sped off to the parking lot at the trailhead where Nick had been seen running the other day. Nick Ballast was an early morning exercise junkie, and I hoped against hope that I'd catch him. I'd screwed him over and I couldn't just let that lie. Especially since the news had probably broken by now. When I parked at the trails, a quick check of my email revealed a *Hollywood Breakdown* news alert. I read the item and it was like a hard kick in the stomach with the heel of a sharp boot: *Nick Ballast Booted from The Weekenders, Replaced by Jenner Davies*.

The news my dad had first heard from my makeup artist mom's friend had made it into print a mere hour later. That's how it worked in Tinsel Town. That's why you had to move quickly if you wanted to make a living reporting, shooting, or following the famous faces that speckled the canvas of Southern California.

The lot was empty, so I stretched and waited. After thirty minutes, Nick pulled up and emerged from the passenger side of a brown Mercedes, sunglasses on. His goateed trainer got out of the driver's side, a Bluetooth tucked on his ear. Nick was laughing and smiling, as if he didn't have a care in the world. He and his trainer headed for the path.

I called out. "Hey, Nick."

The look on his face had turned veiled, unreadable. "Hey," he said. He probably thought I was a fan but couldn't be sure.

"I'm a photographer," I said quickly, and with those words the trainer grabbed the sleeve of Nick's T-shirt and nodded to the path. Because photographers were the bad guys. Nick and his trainer began to jog, but I kept pace as I began my confessional. "I don't have a camera with me now. I'm not here to take a picture. I'm here because I know that Jenner bribed Avery Brock to get your role on *The Weekenders*. He bribed him using photos I took. But I had no idea they were going to be used that way. And if I had, I wouldn't have taken them."

He stopped running. He didn't seem surprised that I'd mentioned the photos of Avery. He seemed intrigued. "But what did you think they were going to be used for?"

His response threw me off. I figured he'd want to know more about the pictures and that he could use my information to get his job back. But instead, his question was inquisitive, it was lawyerly, and it cut me to the core.

"I just thought they'd be used—" I started, but then I stopped. I thought they'd be used on a website or a magazine. I thought they'd be used to titillate the public who craved sordid stories just like I did.

"You thought they'd be used on some gossip site, right?" he fired back. "Whatever these pictures were. You thought they'd just go up online? Just like the pictures of me eating in my car. Did you take those pictures, too?"

I might as well be in the witness box because I was getting a grilling before the jury and I was sure that no twelve people would sympathize with a paparazzo.

"Yes," I said in a small voice. But then I spoke up, because I might be a bottom-feeder on the lowest rung in Hollywood, but I understood Nick. I had the same issues. I wanted him to know I wasn't that different from him. That stars are just like us. Just like me. "I'm sorry. I feel bad for taking those pictures. I know what it's like to battle with food. I've been there myself."

Nick pushed his sunglasses on top of his hair, giving me full view of his green eyes and boyish face. He raised both his hands toward his left shoulder, took out an imaginary bow, and began to play a make-believe violin.

"Too bad you don't have your camera now to get this shot," he said with a full-on sneer of a smile as his violin-playing hand stopped thrumming in time to flip me the bird.

Then he and his trainer left me in the dust.

I turned back the way I came, anger coursing through me as I cursed under my breath like a sailor. I wasn't swearing at Nick, though. Nick had been screwed over, and it had been my fault. Instead, I cursed Jenner, but most of all I cursed myself.

As I reached the parking lot, I forced myself to

cordon off the encounter with Nick. I could wallow in it, or I could keep moving like the other sharks in this town, and there wasn't a choice between the two options. I had to stay strong. I had to stay hungry. I had to keep taking pictures whether the subjects liked it or not. I reminded myself of what J.P. had taught me when I started working for him: *There's a dividing line between celebrities and the rest of us. You stay on your side, Jess, and you never ever apologize for a photo. We're all just trying to make a living in this town.*

I replayed his words, nodding as if he were here giving me a pep talk. I needed a pep talk because I'd started to go soft. But I could put my hard shell back on. I had to live and die in LA.

8

William

After a full morning of being Uncle James's errand boy, a task that entailed picking up his dry cleaning and fetching coffee, I was tired of his runaround. I supposed I shouldn't complain—a job was a job was a job. But yet, he'd shown zero indication that he would sponsor a visa, and sending me out on girl Friday tasks was unlikely to prove my worth.

As I headed to the printer to retrieve a backup of the guest list, I heard James's loud voice from his nearby office.

"Your credentials are great. I'd love to have you come in and we can talk more about the details of working here. We're looking to expand and hire more full-timers and I've been the most impressed with you of all the interviewees," he said, and I nearly stopped in my tracks. I continued very slowly to the printer, so I could hear the rest of his chat.

"Absolutely. Come in Monday and we'll nail down the details."

He hung up as I grabbed the pages. What the hell? I'd been practically begging the bastard for a job, and he'd gone and offered a gig to someone else. Annoyance coursed through me. I couldn't catch a break with him, and he was constantly stringing me along. If he was going to keep teasing me, I'd just as soon cut bait with him.

I popped my head into his office, knocking twice. "Knock, knock."

"Come in, William," he said gruffly, barely glancing up from his computer. "You think you could get me a sandwich soon? My stomach is growling."

Deep breath. Take a deep, calm breath. "Of course. Just let me know what kind. And by the way, I couldn't help but overhear as I was walking down the hall that you're hiring someone. I think that's fantastic, and I'm hoping you might have room here for me, too," I said, gripping the printouts tightly to channel my nerves.

James sighed deeply and looked up at me, scrubbing a hand across his jaw. "Look, kid. I know you're an eager beaver, but here's the thing in the United States. We build ourselves up. We grab our own bootstraps," he said, bending low in his chair and miming yanking on a pair of boots. "That's what I did. I didn't ask for a handout. And I certainly didn't ask my mommy's sister's husband for a job. I built my own damn business, and those are the type of employees I like to hire." I felt my cheeks redden as he cut me down. "You do a fine job installing software and doing records, and hell, I even liked the intel you got me on how the paps work. I'm happy to keep throwing you little jobs here and there. A bit of cash for a couple hours' work. But I just can't get you a full-time job. It's against my moral code."

I nodded crisply, as if I understood the depths of the lesson he thought he was teaching me. Inside, I was burning with frustration. Turning crisp with irritation. This was information he could have shared months ago. Instead, he'd been leading me on the whole time, knowing he was never going to put me on payroll. I opened my mouth to speak and was about to say *thanks for nothing* when I thought of Jess, and the wedding tomorrow. Now was not the time to take a stand. I gulped, rose, and handed him the wedding list. "I completely understand, James. And I respect your morals so much. Now, what kind of sandwich can I get for you?"

"Roast beef with mayo," he said, then returned to his computer without a word.

"Are you bloody fucking kidding me?"

I shook my head as I clutched the phone to my ear on my walk back from the sandwich shop. Traffic chugged along at a usual sluggish pace, even on this side street near James's office. "Wish I was. But nope. The bastard made it patently clear he was never going to hire my sorry, pathetic ass. Have I mentioned again how happy I am that we're not blood relatives to him?"

Matthew laughed lightly, then sighed. "I'm sorry, Will. That totally sucks. I really wish I was in a position to hire you," he said, and I wished that, too. But the harsh reality was that as connected as Matthew and Jane were in the music business, that didn't equate to finding a job only I could do.

"I know. It's okay. I know you've done everything you can," I said, wistfully. Hell, Jane had even tried to make me her personal tech assistant, but the visa-powers-that-be had said that was absolutely a job for an American.

"We won't stop trying. I promise. And listen, I just heard from my editors at *Beat* that I'm flying out tomorrow to LA for an interview with this rising pop band. Let's get together on Sunday morning and we'll brainstorm options for you. We'll see if there are some stones unturned."

A flicker of hope touched down in my chest. I liked my brother, and I always enjoyed seeing him. "That sounds awesome. And maybe you can meet Jess, too."

"Wait," Matthew said, curiosity strewn in his voice. "You did not tell me you were seeing someone."

"Well, I'm telling you now. And she's fantastic."

"Then we really need to find a way for you to stay in the States."

"Exactly," I said, as I neared James's office. I could tolerate two more days working for him for her sake, especially since she was calling me now. "I need to go. That's her on the other line."

"Whipped already," Matthew said, and I could hear the satisfied grin all the way from the other side of the country as he hung up and I answered her call.

"Hey, Jess," I said.

"There's no need to tail Jenner any more," she said, her voice lacking its usual spark as she proceeded to give me all the details of her morning. My jaw nearly dropped with her story, but my mind was quickly turning.

"Here's the thing. I don't think this story ends here," I said.

"Why not?"

"Because what we know is only the outcome—that Jenner's the newest cast member of *The Weekenders* and that Nick's been booted. We don't know how it started. It's as if we have a script with only the second and third acts. Since I know you like to think of everything like a movie script," I said, speaking her favorite language.

"So what happened in the first act?"

"That's what I don't know. But I want to find out, because it could change the ending."

"How?"

"Because we don't know how Jenner could have learned in the first place about Avery hooking up with Riley. How did Jenner, and by extension, the scheming pair of publicist brothers, know that there was something on Avery Brock? Something to blackmail him with. That's the missing link. How Jenner got the tip in the first place," I said as I pushed open the door to James's office. "I need to go, but I'm going to go track this down. And then I'm going to take you out tonight."

"I would like that," she said.

We both would. I might not have had a job, but every day there was more of a reason to stay.

<u>J</u>ess

Six foot five inches of handsome, ripped, muscular man.

Times two.

I could get used to this. I snapped photos of the quarterback of the NFL Renegades team tossing a football on the beach to his star receiver, Jones Beckett. The man could run, he could catch, he could look fantastic in every damn shot.

"Yeah, I can see why you *don't* find him attractive," I whispered to Jillian, who stood next to me, her sleek black hair blowing in the breeze from the ocean.

She pressed her finger to her lips. "Shhh."

"He's so ugly."

"He's the worst."

With dark hair, blue eyes, and a magnetic smile, he was the complete opposite, and he was also a natural in front of the lens. While I loved the celebrity stake-outs, every now and then I enjoyed the pace of a publicity shot like this. There was something rewarding about capturing pics of people who wanted to be photographed.

After I snapped a few more shameless shirtless photos for team publicity, I chatted with Jillian. "Thanks again for giving me the opportunity to work for you," I said, dropping the teasing and sarcasm. I truly did appreciate the chance, and I needed her to know that.

She flashed me a bright smile. "You know you're my girl. How is everything going?"

I caught her up to speed—mostly—on life and classes and work, and then Jones and Cooper joined us.

"Nice work, gentlemen. Should only require minimum photoshopping to make you look like star athletes," I said playfully.

Jones laughed, a rumbly, warm sound. "Good thing you won't have to work too hard."

"Some days it's hardly work," I said.

His eyes strayed to my friend, lingering on her as she brushed her hair from her cheek. "Yeah, I feel that way, too," he said, his voice a little lower.

I watched him, snapping mental shots, as he roamed his gaze over her from head to toe. His eyes were full of heat, full of desire. Whatever was forbidden between them looked like it was about to ignite.

When I grabbed a moment alone with her as we finished, I whispered, "He was completely checking you out. He's into you."

She waved a hand dismissively. "I don't think so."

I nodded. "*Think so.* I promise."

Celebrity dog trainer Claire Tinsley was ready. She was twenty-three and had been born on November 2. She was an organ donor, which was quite thoughtful of her. After an early class, Claire's alter ego had spent the rest of the day after the photo shoot outside the most star-studded Starbucks in the city, snapping latte runs, coffee breaks, and the no-fat frappuccino fixes of the famous. J.P. happily took my work, handed me two hundred dollars, and then gave me the fake ID.

"You look good as a brunette," he said, then gestured to the plate of miniature Meyer lemon cupcakes on his desk. "Take one."

I wrapped a napkin around a cupcake, and J.P. pretended to tip over in his chair and faint from shock.

"What are you doing?"

"I've never seen you take food before. I thought you survived on the blood of celebrities."

"Don't worry. It's not for me."

"For a boyfriend? You holding out on me?"

"Hardly," I lied, but I looked down so he wouldn't

see my eyes as I tucked the wrapped-up cupcake into the front pocket of my backpack.

"You all set for tomorrow? Need anything else?"

I mentally ticked off the pieces I'd need for my wedding costume and the plan to bring my camera inside the event. I'd picked up some wrapping paper at the drug store earlier, along with a pretty white bow, so I even had a gift for the bride and groom. I was good to go, and the twenty-four-hour countdown had started. "I'm ready."

"When do you think I'll see the shots?"

"They're checking cell phones at the gates, so I probably won't be able to get to any sort of device to email you pictures for a couple hours. But by four, for sure."

He rubbed his hands together. "Oh man, I'm like a kid at Christmas. Can. Not. Wait."

"Neither can I," I said, and left J.P.'s office. I stopped at a nearby mall, set up camp on a quiet bench in the courtyard to finish up my bio homework that was due on Monday, and only checked my phone every five minutes for a text from William, so I reasoned that my self-restraint was still strong. I crossed my fingers, hoping he was uncovering the missing scenes—what had happened in the first act.

William

. . .

Things I never want to see on my laptop again—this many photos of Jenner Davies. He dominated my computer screen as I studied image after image of the bleached-blond teen star. There was a shot of him at the soup kitchen on his whole helping-the-less-fortunate quest, then a picture of him visiting sick children, and finally a photo of him cleaning up the beach. But before he became so philanthropic, he was photographed working out quite a bit.

The paparazzi had captured many images of Jenner pumping iron, running on trails, and doing crunches at a gym with his trainer.

I zeroed in on the gym shot because something about it felt eerily familiar, so I stared hard at Jenner as if I could put the pieces together like that. When I glanced away from Jenner's face to take in the rest of the picture, that's when the clue blared loudly at me. His trainer had a goatee. I flashed back to the stakeout with Jess when she'd told me about gym shots, trainers, and Nick Ballast.

His trainer has this goatee, she'd said.

Fine, a lot of guys had goatees. But a lot of guys also *didn't* have goatees. Opening another browser window, I searched for shots of Nick Ballast with his trainer. They showed up immediately, and lo and fucking behold.

Nick Ballast and Jenner Davies had the same personal trainer.

A spark of excitement raced through me.

There it was. The first act. The pieces were coming together.

But then, I told myself to settle down. This didn't prove anything. Lots of trainers had more than one celebrity client. The only way to know if there was anything more to this than mere coincidence was to go to the source.

Since Jess had mentioned the names of some of the most popular gyms in Los Angeles, I looked them up, scrolled through the photos and bios of all the personal trainers, and found him quickly.

His name was Pelly Howland.

I plugged him into Google so I could learn everything about him.

His website popped up. Not an over-the-top one, but it advertised his credentials both as a trainer and in entertainment law. He wasn't a lawyer, but evidently he thought it important to mention in his bio that he'd earned his associate's degree in entertainment law, and was studying now for his bachelor's in the same subject.

Interesting.

Very interesting.

Those details told me *a lot* about him.

As did the fact that his cell phone number was on his page, along with his email. This guy was hungry. He wanted business. Hunger for work was something I knew well. Now I needed to know more about what made Pelly tick, so I turned to Facebook where I discovered that he was quite fond of posting photos of himself while wearing a crisp shirt and tie and sharing status updates from *Hollywood Breakdown*, rather than

dispensing tips about drinking protein shakes after a
workout.

I nodded as the picture of Pelly Howland crystal-
lized. He was a trainer who wanted to be a player.
That's how I would hook him.

Grabbing my phone, I dialed his mobile, but it
went straight to voicemail. "Hi, this is William Oliver,"
I began, opting to use my first and middle name
rather than last. "Heard great things about you from
some of the guys at WAM," I said, tossing out the
name of the biggest talent agency. I didn't say I
worked there. I simply said I'd heard of him from
there, and hoped that would be enough of a lure that
Pelly would feel as if he'd made inroads in the big
beast of Hollywood. "Would love to book a session."

Then I left my number. Next, I tried the gym he
worked at and requested a session with him today.

"He's fully booked. How about next Friday at
9:30?"

"No, thanks," I said, and hung up.

I heaved a frustrated sigh, but remained unde-
terred. There had to be something to the Pelly-Jenner-
Nick connection, and I needed to figure it out. I'd
already discovered that Pelly was social, and active on
Facebook. Maybe he was a Twitter fiend, too. Quickly,
I tracked him down on Twitter, scouring his feed for
any clues. His first update of the day boasted about
working out on the trails. His next claimed he was
booked with sessions all day and *so pumped* for them.
Fine, that was the gist of what I'd learned from the

gym. Then he linked to an article about the potential casting of *We'll Always Have Paris*. One more click of the mouse down his feed, and there it was—an update from twenty minutes ago saying his two p.m. session cancelled but he'd make the most of his free hour with some treadmill time.

Or with me, I reasoned, and hoped Pelly checked his messages in between sessions.

After James's runaround this morning, I refused to let this piece of intel elude me. Determined to snag some face time with the man, I was going to have to try to find him at his gym. I pulled on workout shorts and a T-shirt and hunted around for a Bluetooth headset that had come with my phone but I never wore, seeing as I didn't want to ever look like a douche who wore a Bluetooth except for now when I needed to harness that look. As I opened the door, my phone rang.

"William Oliver," I said.

"Hey! Pelly Howland. I just had a cancellation. You still up for a session? Because I would love to fit you in. I'm all about client service," he said.

"How fortuitous. I'll be there in twenty minutes."

I made my way to Pelly's gym, stopping only at a magazine stand along the way.

I parked a block away from the gym, tucked the headset over my ear, slipped the *Hollywood Breakdown* under my arm, and walked inside, looking the part of a young and hungry Hollywood player, too.

The trainer was waiting for me by the front desk, a

smile on his goateed face. "Pelly Howland, pleasure to meet you."

"William Oliver. And I assure you, the pleasure is all mine," I said, and his eyes stayed on mine at first, then he noticed the *Hollywood Breakdown* in my hand, the Blue-tooth in my ear, and the English accent I'd come equipped with. Not that an accent proved anything in this town, but for some reason, it worked like a fucking charm when you needed someone to think you were trustworthy.

Because after thirty minutes and a few carefully dropped hints that made me seem like a WAM insider, too, my abs were quite sore, and my ears were getting a workout, too.

Pelly the Goateed Trainer was like a windup doll. Crank him up and watch him go. All I had to do was feed him bits and pieces of Hollywood insider intel, and his mouth moved. I dropped names left and right that Jess had mentioned over the last few days.

"You think Emily Hannigan would make a good Gretchen Lindstrom in the *We'll Always Have Paris* remake?" I asked as he made me work my obliques.

"She'd be fantastic, but not opposite Ren Canton."

"Who, then? Someone like Nick Ballast?" I offered in my best casual, offhand tone as we moved onto crunches.

He scoffed, but it was marked with a laugh. "No. Nick is too young for that role."

"He's one of your clients, right?"

Pelly nodded proudly as he held down my ankles. "He is. Damn proud of that kid. He was just cast as a college freshman on a TV show that starts shooting in Vancouver in twelve days."

I mentally pumped a fist, but outwardly kept my cool. "That so? I heard Jenner Davies got Nick's role on *The Weekenders*."

"He's my client, too," Pelly said, and damn, all I had to do was drop a name, and he picked it right up and bragged about it.

"Nick must have been bummed."

Pelly shook his head, and mouthed *no*.

"No?" I whispered in question.

"Nope," Pelly said quietly in a conspiratorial tone. "Nick booked the TV show last week. He wouldn't have been able to do both. The movie shoots here. And the TV show shoots in Canada."

The lights went off. The buzzer beeped. The slot machine played its jackpot tune.

"Ironic that Jenner got the part, then," I mused, going fishing for more. Pelly, it seemed, took the easy bait. So far, I'd pegged him right. He fancied himself a player, some sort of rising power broker.

"Ironic," Pelly said, a note of pride in his voice as he tapped the side of his head. "Or just smart thinking."

"Matchmaking, eh? That's what makes this world go round."

"Yes, it does," Pelly said, and then offered me his hand. "Time for squats."

I counted down until the hour was up. Not because the workout was hard. But because I was dying to tell Jess that our Goateed Trainer Boy was the missing link.

Jess

After a few hours of homework and rampant phone checking, a message came through that William was at a gym and to meet him two blocks away from it by the Santa Monica Pier. The gym was one I'd told him about as a prime paparazzo hangout. I was proud of him for learning the tricks of my trade so quickly.

I packed up my books, popped into the bathroom for a speedy brushing of the teeth—this time I wanted fresh breath for kissing, not for food resistance— and hopped on my scooter to zip west. Twenty minutes later, I found a fast parking spot and locked up my ride. I waved to William as I walked toward him, even though I wanted to launch myself at him since he looked insanely hot leaning against a nearby parking meter, wearing workout clothes—a gray T-shirt and blue nylon shorts. They fit him well, and showed off his strong arms and strong legs, and made my mind trip back to last night because I knew what was inside those shorts. I'd be lying if I said I didn't want to dip my hands beneath the waistband again. I did want to touch him again. He'd felt amazing, and looked so sexy on my couch with his pants down. Actually, I wanted to do more than touch him again. I wanted to know what he tasted like. And there went a hot spark through my body.

Like a shooting star burning me up.

"Hey," I said, trying to sound neutral, as if that would tamp down the lust clouding my brain.

"Hey to you. How was your day?"

"Um. Fine. Yours?"

"It was shitty this morning because my uncle is an ass and there's no chance he's going to hire me," he said.

My heart fell for him. I knew how much he wanted that job. "I'm sorry. That really sucks."

"I know. Trust me, I know."

"But I'm sure you can get something else," I said, trying to sound hopeful because as much as I considered us short-term, there was a part of me that wanted him to stay.

"We'll deal with that another time. Because it's not shitty anymore, since I have good news for you."

Then he told me about his afternoon, every last detail, and I bounced on my toes from the excitement racing through me as I assembled the remaining puzzle pieces. "Are you saying Nick wanted out of the movie to do the show? And Jenner wanted in on anything since he needed a job? And since he and Jenner have the same trainer, the trainer hooked them up with each other and they planned to blackmail Avery Brock together the whole time? That Nick never got the screw? That he actually wanted off the film because he had a better role?" I asked, my brain whirring wildly with the details.

"I'm saying that's an entirely plausible scenario. It answers a lot of questions, doesn't it? Nick and Jenner go to the same gym, they have the same trainer, the trainer is like a good hairdresser and he knows everything about his clients' hopes and dreams, so he sees an opportunity to make a deal. He connects the boys, and there you go. You've got your guy on the inside—Nick. He must have been the one on *The Weekenders* who overheard that Avery was making the moves on Riley, so he and Jenner set up the plan to get the photos with Jenner's publicist. They get the shots, they blackmail Avery, and they get what they want—Nick gets off the movie. Jenner gets on. Nick goes to Canada for a bigger part. Jenner is happy just to have a part. At least that's what I put together with my esteemed private detective skills. Amazing the lengths an actor will go to get or not get a part, isn't it?"

"Amazing, too, how everyone has an agenda," I said, and I didn't have to feel guilty anymore. Nick was a jerk, Jenner was a jerk, Avery was a jerk, and everyone was angling for something. All I had to do was profit from it and shoot it, like J.P. said. I wasn't going to let myself suffer any emotion any more for any actor. They were all jobs to me, and jobs I knew how to do. "Do you know what this means?"

"What does it mean?"

I grinned wildly, and pumped a fist. "It means I don't have to beat myself up about Nick Ballast any more since he engineered the whole damn thing. I didn't screw him over. I didn't make him lose the job. He wanted this to happen, so I don't have to feel guilty about anything any more. Oh, but speaking of guilt, I almost forgot. I have something for you," I said and reached into the front pocket of my backpack. I offered him the cupcake. "I brought this for you. J.P. made it. I hope it didn't get crushed."

"I'd eat it even if it got crushed, and I also won't feel guilty about it at all." He bit into the cupcake. "Damn, that bloke can bake. By the way, I said that for you."

"And it sounded heavenly. *Bloke*," I repeated in a British accent.

"And my stomach thanks you. I've barely had anything to eat today."

"How's that possible? I thought you and food were like this," I said, twisting my index finger around my middle finger.

"This girl I'm working with had me on an all-day stakeout."

"This girl is very impressed with what you learned. And this girl wants to thank you for all that you did."

"Good. Because I want to impress this girl. And I want her to go to the wedding tomorrow, get the pictures, and not feel bad about a damn thing because she shouldn't."

"She's definitely not feeling bad about anything at all right now. In fact, she's thinking about how much she's looking forward to this evening with you."

"Good," he said in an approving voice, pointing to the nearby Santa Monica Pier, with its Ferris wheel and roller coaster. "Do you like roller coasters, by the way?"

"Do I like roller coasters?" I tossed back as if he was crazy for asking. "Do you think there's a chance I don't like roller coasters?"

"I bet you love them," he said, draping an arm around me as we walked. My stomach flipped from the slightest contact. Or maybe it was from the realization that I'd agreed to be his girlfriend last night. That I found myself liking being his girlfriend. We turned onto the pier, strolled along the midway, then past the ring toss and Whac-A-Mole games.

"You know how everyone has an agenda?" he asked.

"Yeah?"

"I have an agenda, too, Dr. Leighton," he said, dropping his arm to my waist and trailing his hand along the small of my back, sending shivers through me. I was putty under his hands. Everything he did melted me from the inside out.

"What's that?"

"To see if you scream on roller coasters or raise your arms in the air."

"Wouldn't you like to know," I answered, returning to our familiar teasing, as we slid into line for the roller coaster. A few minutes later, as the car chugged up the tracks and we rose higher above the Pacific Ocean, I asked William a question. Because I also had an agenda, and now that my life was about to hit smooth sailing, I could go for it.

"Do you remember when I said I wanted to thank you for what you did for me today?"

"Yes. I remember."

"Do you want to know how I want to thank you?" I glanced at him briefly and his eyes said he was damn curious indeed as the car reached the top of the first hill. The sound of wheels cranking along tracks stopped.

There was silence for the briefest of seconds, and in that silence William answered. "I do want to know."

I whispered the answer in his ear.

Then I raised my arms and I screamed.

10

Jess

It didn't take long to make it to William's apartment. I'm pretty sure he set a land speed record on his bike, and I matched his pace. He held my hand as we walked up the stairs, then as he unlocked the door and flicked on the light.

"Here it is, my humble abode," he said, gesturing to his living room. I barely noticed the couch, the table, the kitchen. I had one thing on my mind, and one need in my body.

Him.

"I'll look later," I said, and grabbed his waist and pushed him against the wall.

"Mmm," he moaned appreciatively as I dipped my hands inside his shorts.

"I'm so glad you have workout shorts on. It makes

it so easy to do this," I said, quickly tugging them down to his ankles. His erection sprang free, thick and hard. I wanted to taste him, to touch him, to feel his hands in my hair as he brought me close.

"I aim for easy undressing in moments like this."

I reached for his hard-on, and he drew a sharp breath as my fingers wrapped around him. He rocked into my palm, his breath already speeding up and I hadn't even taken him in my mouth yet as I planned to. But I was about to.

"William," I whispered.

He opened his stormy gray eyes. They were hazy with desire.

"You know how I said this was a thank you?"

"Yes."

I shook my head. "It's not a thank you. I'd never do this to say thank you. I'm doing it because I want to."

Then he grabbed my hair and tugged me in close for a searingly hot kiss, exploring my mouth and devouring my lips, all while he grew even harder in my hand. I broke the kiss and dropped down to my knees.

"Incidentally, that was the hottest thing you've ever said," he said, and then we both stopped talking when I kissed him, then inch by delicious inch I took him in further. He made the sexiest sounds, groaning as he speared his fingers through my hair. He grew harder and thicker in my mouth. At first he watched me, his heated gaze focused on my lips, but soon his eyes floated closed and his moans turned louder. They drove me on.

With my lips wrapped around him, and my tongue trailing up and down, I enjoyed every single second of his pleasure.

Thank you very much.

William

"I lied."

"What do you mean?" I asked Jess a few minutes later as we sank down onto my couch.

"I do have a thank you present for you."

I raised my eyebrows in question, as she stretched across me to reach into her backpack for a small white box.

As she held it in her lap, she fiddled with the corners. My heart beat faster knowing she was nervous. It was adorable and intoxicating all at once, and it made me want to kiss away her nerves. But then, most things she did made me want to kiss her. Come to think of it, I pretty much wanted to touch her all the time. Twenty-four seven. With breaks only for pizza.

"I thought you could wear this to the wedding. Since it's a pretty fancy date for us," she said, and I swore the tiniest bit of red spread across her cheeks. I'd never seen Jess blush before. She wasn't the blushing kind.

She handed me the box.

"My first gift from you. I will treasure it, whatever

it is," I said, and pressed a soft kiss to her forehead that seemed to ease her nerves. I opened the box to find a pair of cuff links inside. They were some kind of brushed metal and looked like miniature padlocks. "They're lovely."

"I asked my brother to send them. His company makes them from recycled materials, and these are created from the padlocks that people put on the bridges in Paris. He has a deal with the city of Paris, which has far too many locks on the bridges now. He takes the used padlocks and makes them into these beautiful cuff links. And I thought if you're going to a wedding, you might as well have cuff links. So thank you so very much for allowing me to be your wedding date," she said, and her lips curved up into a pretty smile, one that said she was happy not only to be crashing the wedding, but to be doing so with me.

I ran my finger over the cuff links, then set the box aside. "They're gorgeous, and it will be an honor to wear them tomorrow. And an even bigger honor that you are my date."

"You know, William," she said as she trailed her hands along my arm. "We should watch *Anyone's Dough* sometime. Since that was the first movie we bonded over."

"We should. But it's going to be a long, long time before we get to it because I'm much more interested in doing other things with you."

"Me, too," she said with a sly wink.

Then I kissed her for a long, long time.

SATURDAY

SATURDAY

Weather: 70 degrees, Sunny

11

I would miss my cell phone. I kissed the screen good-bye, powered it off, and tucked it away in my desk drawer. A phone with all your contacts and access to your email is not something you want to chance losing, even if you have a secret storage area under the seat of your scooter. Besides, I'd picked up a dumb phone at the convenience store for twenty dollars. William and Anaka were the only ones with the direct number. He was already at the event—he'd had an early morning arrival time at the grounds, he'd told me.

I slung my heavy backpack, filled with my dress, my wig, my shoes, the purse, and the wedding gift onto my shoulders, and popped into Anaka's room to say goodbye. Lying on her belly, decked out in a bright orange top, a miniskirt, and gray-and-orange striped knee-high socks, she was tapping away on her laptop.

"Jess! I'm working on my screenplay," she said, beaming at me.

"Good. I figured that would be the only reason you'd be up this early on a Saturday."

"It's coming along. I'm right at the part where there's a big misunderstanding."

"And does everything fall to pieces and the audience thinks there's no chance in hell for the leads to ever work out their problems?"

She nodded, a pleased look on her face. "Of course. I want to devastate the audience."

"Perfect, because they want to be devastated."

"Have you got the dress I left you for the wedding?" she asked. Anaka had loaned me one of the dresses she wore to charity functions with her parents since I didn't have the type of attire a guest would usually wear to a celebrity wedding.

I nodded. "It's folded carefully in my bag. I'm going to change into it when I get closer."

"If you see my dad, look away," she teased, since her father was on the guest list.

"Here's hoping he doesn't recognize me in my wig. But I will do my best to steer clear of him. Text me if you need anything."

"Same for you. I'm heading to my parents' house to do my laundry since they won't be there the rest of the day," she said. Saturday was laundry day for Anaka, and since she was particular about her wardrobe, she preferred to use her mother's washer and dryer, with all the fancy settings and special cycles.

"Be sure the neighbors don't spot you air-drying your lacy underthings on the deck," I said with a wink, and she laughed. "By the way, did you ever get the details from your cousin on her romantic entanglements?"

Anaka rolled her eyes. "She's being super evasive. She just keeps saying *it's complicated*. I'm going to have to stop texting and resort to calling."

"Such an old-fashioned way of communicating," I said.

Then I was off, flying down the highway, weaving in and out of cars, on my way to the wedding that would change my life. I didn't feel guilty any more either. I only felt a twinge of early victory. My heart beat faster, and I was bursting with anticipation and the kind of jumpy, happy jitters that precede a Christmas morning. This was it. This was my moment. My big shot. Everything had been planned perfectly.

I signaled, turned off the highway at the Ojai Ranch exit, and drove down the main drag in pursuit of a branch of the local public library near Chelsea Knox's estate. I'd looked it up online, but I'd also seen plenty of photos of Chelsea reading picture books to her young children from the comfort of the beanbags in the kids' reading room.

Pulling into the parking lot, I locked my scooter and headed inside. Libraries happened to have much nicer public restrooms than Starbucks did.

Inside the stall, I changed from my jeans, Converse sneakers, and T-shirt into the classy navy-blue dress from Anaka, along with beige pumps and the matching beige purse. I brushed out my blond hair, looped it into a low ponytail, then pulled it into a stocking cap. The wig went on next, and I adjusted the edges near my ears, so I'd look like a natural brunette. I folded my clothes, stuffed them in my backpack, and left the stall. At the mirror, I touched up my makeup, kicking it up a notch from my usual look, making my lashes longer and my lips a shade of light pink, outlined in a darker pink with lipliner. I was ready for a wedding. More important, I was ready to go earn my medical school bills for the next year or so. At precisely two o'clock when Veronica Belle walked down the aisle to the theme music from *SurfGhost* and pledged to honor, cherish, and adore Bradley Bowman for the rest of her life, I'd have everything I needed for my future.

I left the library, zoomed 1.7 miles to the road that led to Chelsea's home, and cut the engine, parking my scooter near the cars of the other wedding guests. A twenty-something woman in a pale yellow dress stepped out of the car next to me, and said hello.

"Hi," I replied. I didn't recognize her, but not everyone attending was famous. Claire Tinsley certainly wasn't. I stuffed my backpack under the seat of my scooter, locked the seat, slid my purse on my arm, and held the box with the wedding gift inside it, wrapped neatly in white paper with raised white bells and a bow that would never come undone. My wallet with my fake ID was inside the purse. I checked my dumb phone one last time as I walked to the line of guests at the gate.

There was a new text from William.

Change of plans.

I froze when I saw those three words. I pressed hard on the middle button on the phone to call up the rest of the message. These dumb phones were slow.

I breathed easily again when I read the rest of the message. *Just wanted to let you know no one's checking IDs any more for the app. All you have to do is give your name. They'll check the list. Claire's on it. James is running me around like crazy so I'll try to find you when I can.*

That was a relief. But yet it was strange. After all the security precautions, the leaks planted about the false locations, as well as the plainclothes security all over the grounds, why would Veronica no longer want the guest list verified?

The girl in the yellow dress gave the security guy her name, and handed over her cell phone.

I closed William's message, and saw one from Anaka had just arrived. Only the first few words appeared on the screen. *Um, my dad's not—*

But the message cut off, and as I stabbed the middle button to open the note, the security guard had already nodded to the woman in the yellow dress and motioned for her to head to the nearby golf cart, waiting to ferry guests from the gate to the house.

I closed the phone before I could read Anaka's message.

"Hi. I'm Claire Tinsley," I said, and my voice

sounded scratchy and gravelly. I was trying to sound different, to throw them off the scent. But that was silly, I reminded myself. I needed to not stand out.

The security guard—Sal, I remembered, since William had told me his name—ran his index finger down the paper. My lungs threatened to leap out of my body as he scanned. I didn't see Claire's name on the list. My heart was planning a mutiny as he turned to the next page. My name was always near the middle of any list. Where could it be? Then my insides settled and I remembered why. Because my last name usually started with an *L*. But today it started with a *T*.

The security guard found Claire Tinsley's name, then asked for my cell phone. I handed it to him, and he wrote my name on masking tape, then pressed the tape onto the phone. He looked through my purse, patting my wallet and my makeup case. He waved me in. "There's a table for presents right inside the front door."

"Thank you," I squeaked out, as I took a seat next to Yellow Dress in the golf cart. I held on tight to the gift.

That was it. It was so easy, it was beyond easy. I was inside the premises, and now all I had to do was assemble the camera when I reached the house.

"Friend of the bride? Or friend of the groom?"

Yellow Dress was making small talk as the cart bumped over the driveway.

"Bride," I said in my normal voice this time. "You?"

"Same. We went to college together," she said, a cheery smile on her face.

"Oh, that's nice. What did you study?"

"English literature," she said. "What about you? How do you know Veronica?"

Yellow Dress seemed to be studying me closely, and I worried she might recognize me from the photos with Riley and Sparky McDoodle from earlier in the week. But my dog alibi fit that, too.

"I'm a dog trainer. I've worked with the family's Chihuahua–mini pins."

"Oh my God. That is such a coincidence. I have to ask you a dog question. My Yorkie won't stop getting into the cat's food, and I feed the cat in the laundry room. I'm so worried he's going to get fat."

I nodded several times, playing the part of the cool, confident dog trainer who'd dealt with this situation before. I flicked back to the episodes I'd watched of *I'm a Dog Person* while training Jennifer. "What you need to do in those situations is set a trap for the dog. You have to leave the door to the laundry room open, set the food there for him, and just wait. When he makes a move for it, then you correct him."

"Interesting," she said with wide and curious eyes. "Do I just give him a sharp *no*?"

I nodded with authority. "Yes. Or else you get a training collar."

She shook her head, her eyes showing fear. "A training collar? Like the kind that pinches them? I don't want to hurt him."

"Of course you don't. But you certainly don't want him to get fat, either, do you?"

"That's true. I definitely don't want a fat dog," she said with such supreme worry in her voice that it had to be genuine. We arrived at the house. "You were so helpful. Thank you."

I let her go ahead of me, and when I walked through the door a minute later, I took mental photos of Chelsea Knox's palatial *and* eco-friendly entryway, noting the solar panels high above in the arched roof and the furniture made from renewable materials in the living room. Next to the door was a table stacked with gifts. I turned sharply to my left, and into the first bathroom in the hallway. I closed the door quickly, locked it, and opened the wedding gift. I'd wrapped it TV-style, which meant I didn't have to unwrap it. I simply lifted the wrapped top off the box.

Inside the box was my gorgeous camera. After setting it on the counter next to the sink, I put the cover to the gift back on. Next, I unzipped my purse, and retrieved the big makeup tub that had once held copious amounts of powder. Now, the makeup tin held the lens to my camera. I removed the lens and nested it on the camera. Then, I reached into the bag and yanked off the masking tape that had kept a circular section of fabric in place. As planned, there was now a hole in the side of the bag precisely the size and shape of the end of a lens of a camera. Carefully placing the camera inside the purse, I positioned it so the lens lined up with the hole. Then I took scotch tape from a zippered compartment and used it to re-tape the circle of fabric back onto the lens from the outside, so the bag wouldn't look suspicious. Returning the scotch tape to the compartment, I double- and triple-checked the placement of the camera, then shut the purse and pulled it onto my shoulder, keeping the side with the circular, taped-on cutout against my body.

As I checked my reflection in the mirror, I noticed I was shaking. I took a deep breath, my shoulders rising up and down. The air filled my lungs, calming me. After several more breaths, I felt settled again and ready. I looked at my watch—1:39. Showtime was in twenty-one minutes.

Tucking the empty gift under my arm, I unlocked the bathroom door and nearly jumped when I opened it. William was waiting on the other side.

"You scared me," I whispered, my heart pounding fast in my chest.

"Would you like me to take the gift for Ms. Belle and Mr. Bowman?" he said with an easy smile, one that suggested we were co-conspirators. "I can bring it to the table if you'd like."

"I would like that very much." I handed him the wrapped and empty box.

Then he scanned the hallway. Guests were still entering the house, so he leaned in close to my ear, so only I could hear. "I need to run. James has me doing a ton of stuff all over. But I can't wait to see you later."

"Me, too," I said, then he turned away.

I walked to the backyard, wishing I could snap photos of everything along the way, from the back deck that wrapped around the house, to the yoga sanctuary beyond the deck, to the garden full of organic vegetables and fruit that Chelsea claimed to tend and harvest herself.

Instead, I was a good girl, and I headed to the folding white chairs set up underneath the tent and beside the mechanical koi pond. Standing vases of daisies and sunflowers, Veronica's two favorite varieties of flowers, lined the aisles. A long white runner led from the back steps of the house all the way to the makeshift altar under the bamboo veranda where Sandy, the talk show host, would soon officiate. An usher led me to a chair about two-thirds of the way from the altar. I sat next to a woman in a red slinky dress and a man in khaki pants. I didn't know them.

A string quartet by the altar played classical music.

I held my purse tightly and checked my watch. The ceremony would start in thirteen minutes. I looked around, trying to spot faces as the chairs filled up. Everyone looked vaguely familiar. Everyone looked vaguely pretty and reasonably attractive in a random sort of way. But no face stood out. No features brought instant recognition.

Perhaps the famous guests were waiting until the last minute. Perhaps they'd swoop in and fill the empty seats mere seconds before the bride walked down the aisle. But I flashed back to the half-read text message from Anaka—*Um, my dad's not*—and figured she must have been trying to tell me her dad wasn't coming. Why wouldn't he be here? Why would he have a last-minute change of plans and miss the wedding?

I tried to dismiss the flight of nerves that circled me.

Soon, the officiant walked out of the house. She had the same cropped blond hair as the TV talk show host, but she definitely wasn't Sandy. That was odd. Next came the groom, slipping around the chairs so he wouldn't disturb the runner for his bride. I watched him, and something seemed off about his stride, but I could only see him from the back. Several groomsmen followed and they assumed their posts in front of the guests, and I could have sworn from where I sat that Bradley Bowman had more chiseled cheekbones. Even so, I opened my bag, rooted around as if I were looking for a tissue, and kept my right hand inside the bag to operate the camera. With my left hand, I removed the fabric cutout for the lens, freeing the camera to capture the event. I lifted the purse higher, holding it against my chest. I pushed the silver button on the camera several times to capture Bradley as he waited for his bride.

Then Pachelbel's Canon began, and everyone turned their heads to watch the bride. Clutching my purse for dear life, I shifted, too, and kept snapping surreptitiously as the bridesmaids walked down the aisle.

The only trouble was, the bridesmaids weren't Chelsea, or Veronica's best friend, or Riley Belle.

Nor was the bride Veronica Belle. My heart sank and my skin burned the furious red of self-loathing when I realized why I hadn't spotted a single familiar face among the guests. Everyone here was an actor.

Everyone was a stand-in. Everyone was faking it. That's why no one needed to check IDs after all.

Veronica Belle had staged a decoy wedding, and I'd fallen hard for it. I had the worthless photos to prove it.

12

Jess

I cried stupid tears all the way to the library, wiping the streaky lines of mascara roughly from my cheeks. But more leaked out, a cocktail of anger and self-loathing. I'd been greedy, and I'd been foolish, and that was a dangerous combination. I pulled into the library lot, almost toppling my scooter through my blurry, rage-y haze. When I jumped off, I caught a corner of the navy-blue dress on the metal covering of the wheel. I yanked until the fabric came free, tearing the skirt in a slash up the thigh.

Curses flew from my mouth. Enough to send truckers covering their ears.

Frustration poured through every cell in my body. Nothing was going right today, and now I'd owe Anaka a new dress. Hastily, I grabbed my backpack from under the seat, and marched inside to my changing room.

I tugged the dress over my head in one clunky motion, stopping only to wipe more wetness from my eyes. The dress was useless now, so I pressed the fabric against my face, as if I could stopper all the sadness. But I had no right to cry, no decent reason to feel so indignant. This was a job, and the job hadn't come through as advertised. It was only money. I should know better than to cry over money.

There.

Sucking in the last of the tears, I stuffed my wig into my backpack and returned to my regular clothes. When I left the stall, I turned on the cold water in the sink and splashed some on my face. I peered into the mirror and administered a dose of much-needed self-medication: "Get yourself together, Jess. Big girls don't cry."

I let the bathroom door fall behind me, and was about to put Ojai Ranch as far in the rearview mirror as I could, when I heard two librarians at the front counter whispering to each other.

"You have to see these pictures. They just showed up on *On the Surface* a minute ago."

My spine tingled. I stopped at the closest shelf of books, and pretended to look through the new releases as I listened.

"Oh. My. God," the younger of the two women said, stopping at each high-pitched word to catch a breath. "They eloped!"

The floor gave out. My vision went fuzzy.

Reaching for the gray metal shelf of books, I steadied myself. I'd never felt faint before, but I gripped the metal tight till the moment passed. Then I stopped pretending to listen in, and walked straight over to the counter.

"Sorry to interrupt, but I couldn't help but over-hear that someone had eloped," I started, quickly recovering as I did my best to appear calm.

The woman smiled, and her hazel eyes lit up. This was a moment not to be missed—the delicious moment when celebrity news that surprised everyone began spreading across the Internet. She swiveled her computer monitor around to show me the site.

"Veronica Belle and Bradley Bowman eloped to Las Vegas!" She squealed. "They tied the knot literally thirty minutes ago. Can you believe it? They went to an Elvis-themed wedding chapel with just their family members."

The floor tilted once more and the sickening feeling hit my stomach. I stared hard at the pictures on the screen of Veronica in a sassy white minidress and Bradley in shorts and a short-sleeve button-down. They were laughing as they left the chapel, two sets of parents and a few pairs of siblings behind them. Everyone was dressed in casual wear, including the sister of the bride in a cute miniskirt, clutching Sparky McDoodle in her arms as she smiled brightly. The next shot showed Veronica tossing a tiny bouquet of daisies behind her. Then there was a picture of the newlyweds and their families hopping into a black stretch limo.

Flash.

The pictures had to have been taken by Flash. She was always one step ahead of me. Now she was three hundred miles ahead of me in Las Vegas, and probably laughing and smiling as she counted to one hundred thousand.

I swallowed thickly, trying to push down this terrible taste of failure in my mouth.

"That is just so clever," the librarian said, and I realized she'd been speaking the whole time. "We were just talking about how something must have been happening down at Chelsea's home today. I saw the party rental trucks, and then there were florist vans and a big red car that had some caterer's name on it. What was that all about?" she asked with a kind of awestruck curiosity.

Her friend answered. "It must have been a decoy wedding."

The redhead laughed, as if such a stunt was the most clever thing she'd ever heard.

"Yeah, it was," I said in in a dead voice. "They hired actors. Extra types to show up. Pretend to be guests. Fill the seats. They even had stand-ins for Veronica and Bradley and Chelsea and Riley. They had security, too. To make it all seem real."

"That is amazing to go to that effort. To spend all that money to just throw paparazzi off the scent," the redhead said in admiration.

Her friend chimed in. "Well, nobody likes the paparazzi."

Truer words were never spoken, and on that note,

I left and drove all the way home without looking back.

13

William

Stuck on the other side of the property manning the front door of the estate, I barely even caught a glimpse of her leaving, just a flurry of color—her navy dress, her brown wig, her beige purse, and then, like a mirage in the desert, she was gone.

Minutes later, I was momentarily freed, so I tried calling several times, but her phone rang and rang. I swore under my breath, then with my focus on the gates, I picked up the pace, eager to search for her phone. She'd probably left it behind.

But James corralled me on the way and cut me off, "Change of plans," he barked. "I need you over there in the receiving line. Congratulate the bride and groom."

I tilted my head, as if I could better decipher his request from an angle. "But—" I started. "What's the point?"

"No buts," he hissed. "It's part of the job."

"Did you know it was a fake wedding?" I asked in a harsh clip, because he'd screwed over Jess. Big time.

He gave me a look like he thought I was stupid. "Kid, they're my clients. Of course I knew."

"And you didn't mention it?" I asked, as if I were a lawyer in a courtroom, quizzing a belligerent witness. I reminded myself that whether he was in on it or not, he never knew I was the man on the inside, sneaking in a paparazzo to take clandestine shots. Truth be told, I hadn't a leg to stand on when it came to this moral battle. Still, I was pissed as hell, and keeping me in the dark *felt* wrong.

"Don't get your panties all bunched up because you missed the chance to meet Veronica and Bradley. You'll get used to it in Hollywood," James said, clapping me on the back.

Fighting the urge to roll my eyes and bite out a sarcastic comment, I drew a quick, deep breath, plastered on a smile, and said, "I assure you, that's not the case."

He stared down at me with wide and annoyed eyes. "Then get back out there and mingle. That's the job, kid. We've got to keep up the appearance. That's what the client wants. Eat some kale, look like a guest, then be on your merry way. Look, I know you're hunting for a job, and I'm sorry as hell I can't give you one, but do me a solid here and finish this up today, then tomorrow we'll meet with the publicity shop about the paparazzi intel you got for me, and if you do those things, I'll be sure to give you a good recommendation as you look for work, maybe even refer you to a few friends. How about that?"

He looked me square in the eyes, knowing he had something I wanted. Maybe it wasn't a job, but it was something I'd need for another one. A positive recommendation could make the difference in landing a gig in the next two months.

"Fine," I muttered.

Shoving me on the shoulder, James whispered, "Go."

I headed to the line of wedding guests, who were clearly actors, along with the stand-ins for Veronica and Bradley. Taking my turn behind a sea of players, I waited under the hot sun by the back deck, willing the line to move faster so I could escape and track down Jess.

When I reached the wedding party, the fake Bradley extended his hand. "Thank you so much for attending," he said.

"We're so glad you're here," fake Veronica echoed.

"Pleasure to be here. What a lovely ceremony, and such beautiful grounds," I said, and the moment was beyond false, even by Hollywood standards.

"I'm thrilled you enjoyed it," fake Bradley said, never once breaking character. It was like being at an interactive dinner theater. "Please, have some appetizers," he added, gesturing to the nearby waiters circling with trays of small food.

As I walked away, a waiter offered me kale-wrapped asparagus spears, but I shook my head. I spent the next hour logging every detail of the fake wedding. At least I'd have that info to share with Jess. Not that it amounted to much, but it was the only thing I had to offer her. She'd done her part and given me the intel I needed for James. That he hadn't hired me wasn't her fault. But I'd come up short for her. A heavy stone settled in my stomach knowing I'd failed to deliver my half of the deal.

Jess

Anaka waggled the two pints in front of me. "Are you sure you don't want gelato? My mom has Talenti's Caribbean Dream and Caramel Salt Crunch."

I waved her off. "I will eat all of them," I said, as I laid on the cool tiled kitchen floor at Anaka's parents' house.

"That's the point. I think you need a pig-out session right now."

"Then I will yak up every last ounce. Maybe even eat the container, too, and I'll barf that as well, and then your mom's cat would eat that."

"Then I'm glad you warned me. I won't waste the good gelato on comforting you," she said, and closed the sub-zero freezer. She sat down on the floor, cross-legged next to me. When Anaka had arrived at her parents' house earlier in the day with her laundry in tow, she'd been expecting an empty home. Instead, she was greeted by her mom still in her tennis skirt when they were supposed to have been getting ready for a wedding.

"I'm heading out for a tennis lesson and your father booked a last-minute afternoon tee time," Anaka's mother told her, then clued her in on the whole ruse. That's when Anaka had rushed to her phone to text me, but I hadn't been able to get to the message in time. Not that it would have mattered. I'd already been fooled. I was a fool.

Her dad received the alert from the Bowman-Belle camp a few days ago that the Ojai Ranch setup was just that. That the couple was eloping, and he could return his tux to his closet. Everyone who was on the real guest list received the alert, too. The couple waited until only a few days before to tell their friends because they wanted the elopement to be as secret as it could possibly be. They wanted their wedding on their terms.

I couldn't fault them, especially given how they'd outsmarted everyone but Flash. Deep pockets made for easy outsmarting. They had the resources to stage a fake wedding, all for the simple pleasure of enjoying a real one. A quiet one.

A wedding for their eyes only.

"How do you think the pictures of their real wedding showed up on the tabloids?" I asked.

Anaka furrowed her brow for a few seconds, then snapped her fingers. "You said that other photographer was at the bridesmaid fitting? Taking pictures there?"

I nodded.

"I bet she overheard something then," Anaka suggested, and I nodded. That seemed plausible enough. Clearly, Flash had heard about the wedding somehow. Flash was at the top of her game. She had her ear to the ground, she was fast, and she had good sources, judging from all the times I ran into her on the job.

"What am I going to do now?" I moaned.

"Same thing you've always done."

"What's that? Be a pain in the butt? Be annoying and tightly wound and take stupid pictures of celebrities who are smarter than me?"

"You got outsmarted once. Big deal. You just keep on going," she said in the most matter-of-fact tone possible.

"How am I going to pay for medical school?" I whined.

"You do have ten thousand dollars from Keats, as well as the money you've been earning from your job, right?"

"Yes," I grumbled, because I wasn't facing a zero balance. I wasn't rolling in it, but I had a few bucks to start with.

"It's something, Jess. It's something," she said, punching me lightly on the shoulder in an encouraging gesture.

I breathed out hard. "Yeah, but I need more to pay the first year's tuition bill. What am I supposed to do?" I held my hands out wide, probably looking like I was making snow angels on the floor.

"You'll just have to do what everyone else does. You keep working, you get some loans, and you deal."

If she were anyone else, I'd say *easy for you to say*. Her college was all paid for and then some. But I'd never fault Anaka for coming from means, just as she'd never mock me for not. We understood each other. We understood where we were different, and where we were the same.

"Besides, if all else fails, you can just be a plastic surgeon. You'll repay the loans like that," she said, and snapped her fingers.

I rolled my eyes. "Because there's no competition in LA at all for plastic surgeons."

"Just look on the bright side. At least you have a date tonight with a hot guy."

I propped myself up on my elbow. "Speaking of, do you think William was in on it? Do you think he knew about it and set me up?"

Her jaw dropped as she rolled her eyes. "Are you auditioning for the role of world's leading conspiracy theorist?"

"No! But come on," I asked, furrowing my brow. "Are you telling me the caterers, the party rental people, the security firm didn't know it was a hoax?"

"Jess, my love, think about this like a screenplay. If you were trying to pull off a big super-secret con, would you tell as many people or as few people as possible?"

I shrugged. "He could have known. I mean, he hasn't called. He was probably using me all along."

"Pretty sure he hasn't called because you don't have your phone. Do you want to bet you have a dozen missed calls on your phone when you get home?"

"Sure. I'll bet you a hundred thousand dollars," I said, and managed a small laugh.

"Oh, I'm going to collect because I know he's calling."

We stayed like that for a few more minutes, chatting about everything and nothing, as we always did, and Anaka made me laugh once more when she tracked down her mom's Siamese cat, Suede, and showed me how she'd taught him to fetch a ball of crumpled-up tinfoil, return it, then fetch it again. Soon, her phone rang. She reached for it, checked out the number, and said to me, "I have no idea who this is." Then into the phone, "Hello?"

Silence filled the air, as a knowing smile spread across her face. As her eyes sparkled. As she adopted a look that said she was going to collect on our one hundred thousand dollar bet.

"Hi, William," she said loudly. "She's right here."

She handed me the phone.

"Jess, are you okay?" he asked, and his voice was like a massage. Instantly, it relaxed me and somehow made me feel as if the world wasn't upside down.

"Yeah," I said heavily.

"I tried calling you but it just rang and rang and rang. And you didn't have your regular phone, and you didn't take your other phone when you left. I had literally no idea it was a fake wedding. You have to know that. James never told me until after the ceremony. Remember when I told you that we weren't allowed to go near the room Veronica was getting ready in?"

I flashed back to our stakeout of Riley and Avery, when he'd shared the blueprints. "Yes."

"That was why, evidently. They staged it all. And I'm so sorry you didn't get the pictures you wanted. I feel terrible," he said in a soft and sweet voice that very nearly melted me into a puddle on Anaka's kitchen floor. That damn accent was still working its charms.

"Me, too. How did you get Anaka's number?"

"After James had me running this way and that, I was finally able to get away, so I went to the security table at the gate, and I went through the whole box of phones and found the one you'd been using. There were only two numbers on it. Mine and Anaka's. I called hers. Since I knew you weren't at my number," he said, and I could practically see the knowing grin curve up on his lips. He always knew how to make me laugh, and make me smile. "Where are you right now?"

"I'm at Anaka's house."

"Can I come see you?"

I turned to Anaka. "Can William come over?"

She swatted me. "Are we four years old? Of course."

She grabbed the phone, and gave him directions.

"I've been dying to meet you all week since she told me you were constitutionally good-looking. *Her words.*"

Then when she hung up, I shrugged. "It's true. You're going to wish he were yours," I said, as my lips twitched in a smile. At least, there was that. He was mine. For now.

14

Jess

"They still served cake?" Anaka asked, shocked, as she tucked her feet underneath her.

William sat in a cushiony chair across from us, still decked out in his wedding attire, but with a few buttons undone on his white dress shirt. Anaka and I were stationed on the pale blue couch in the living room, and she demanded a chapter and verse rundown on what had gone down after the exchange of the *I dos*, which marked precisely the moment I had taken off.

"Yes. But it was gluten-free cake. And they served all the food, too—kale, carrots, and quinoa salad. Chelsea Knox is this big environmentalist, so she probably didn't want to waste anything. They'd ordered all the food already."

"God forbid they waste gluten-free cake. Talk about yakking up food," Anaka said, and mimed gagging. "That shit is nasty."

"Stop. This whole conversation is giving me a headache," I said and pressed a hand to my forehead.

Anaka was not deterred. "Were there other paparazzi there?"

William nodded. "At the end, word got out that it was faked so there were a few photogs out on the street near her driveway. Someone tried to climb the fence apparently."

After a few more questions, Anaka brushed one palm against the other. "Well, I have a load of delicates that need tending to, and then I just had this strange notion—maybe it landed out of the blue—that I've been missing Suede so much I'm going to sleep at my parents' house and cuddle with the family cat tonight," she said, then squeezed my shoulder and winked.

I pulled her in for a hug. "Suede is going to be so happy," I said, teasing her.

"Get out of here, and go enjoy this very good thing you have, rather than thinking about what you don't have," she whispered in my ear.

After she said goodbye at her parents' front door, we walked along her circular driveway to where our respective rides were parked—his motorcycle and my scooter.

I rested my hand on the handlebars, and William stood next to me.

"So," he said, waiting for me to say what happens next.

"So."

"Jess, I'm really sorry about the wedding."

Jutting up my shoulders, I shot him a rueful smile. "Me, too. But what about you? Do you still need intel from me? For that publicist client?"

"James wants me to come to one last meeting with the client tomorrow, and then I'm done with him. Though he is giving me a nice recommendation so I couldn't tell him off with a grand *I quit* like they'd do in the movies."

"That's absolutely how they'd do it in the movies," I said, cracking a small smile. "I hate it when life doesn't work like the movies. Sorry things with James aren't panning out."

"Truth be told, he's such a dick that I suppose it's all for the best, and I'll simply have to look elsewhere for a job."

"I'll help you. However I can," I offered.

He took a step closer. "You would?" he said as he touched my cheek with his thumb, tracing the outline of my jaw.

"Of course. I don't know how, but we'll figure something out. Because I really want you to——" I let my voice trail off. Vulnerability was far too uncomfortable a coat to wear. But even so, I had to find the guts to say what I wanted. I had to, every now and then, let go of the way I kept people at a distance. The more I tried to control things, the less I was able to.

"To?" he prompted.

I swallowed down my fear, letting my chest fill only with the strange certainty I felt for him. For us. We were both so disappointed today, so let down in our quests. But at least we had *this*. Each other. We didn't find what we were looking for, but we had somehow found something else other than work or money. "To stay," I said, keeping my gaze locked on his the whole time, watching his eyes light up with my words.

"Me, too. So much," he said, lacing his hands through my hair and pressing his forehead to mine.

I didn't know what to say with his hands in my hair. It felt too good for words.

"What now?" he asked softly. "No one to follow. No elaborate spy acrobatics to plan."

"No agenda," I said, continuing.

"Nothing but the present," he said. "What should we do?"

I didn't answer that question. Instead, I pulled back to look into those stormy gray eyes. My lips parted, and my chest rose and fell, and I tried to find a way to restore speech. I hoped he could read my mind, or my body language, as I angled closer to him, but I was sure we were on the same page. I went for it.

"I think this is the moment in the script where the heroine invites the hero to spend the night," I said.

He hitched in a breath. "It's only afternoon," he said, his voice hot against my skin.

"Late afternoon," I amended.

He ran the pad of his thumb across my top lip, and I shivered. "Then this is the moment where the hero says yes."

He lifted my chin and dropped his mouth to mine. We kissed for many minutes that folded into themselves, and in the span of the kiss, I didn't think about money or medical school or pictures. I didn't linger on a single thing except his lips, and his hair, and his hands, and the astonishing closeness of his body.

He pulled away for a second. "Let's go now. I want the rest of the night to start immediately."

We put on helmets and he rode behind me all the way to my apartment.

We started on the couch. For the simplest of reasons. The bedroom was too far away. As soon as we tumbled through the door, his hands were on my waist and slinking under my shirt, and my breath was already coming fast. I tugged him down on me on the couch, thrilling at the way his long, strong body felt on top of mine. Of course, I already knew how he felt on top of me, but now I was going to know the feel of him in a whole new way, and goosebumps rose on my skin with the anticipation.

His lips found mine once more and he kissed me hungrily, making the sexiest groans as he nibbled on my lips and then explored my mouth. When we pulled apart for air, I pressed my hands to his chest and looked at him. "I think you're addicted to kissing me," I said playfully.

"So unbelievably addicted to kissing you," he said, a wicked glint in his eyes, as he bent his head to my neck, blazing a trail of kisses up to my ear. "I want to kiss you in other places," he said, his ravenous words making my stomach flip.

"Where?" I asked, knowing the answer, but dying to hear it from him.

"Between your legs. I'm dying to taste you," he said with a heady groan as he lowered his hand to my jeans and palmed me where I was hot for him. In an instant, I responded, his touch heating me up more. I rocked into his hand.

"I want that, William. I want that so much," I said, my breathing already speeding up to a wild pace.

"Let me take your clothes off," he said, his voice barren against the silence of the apartment. That's when it hit me—a little mood music would be nice.

"Hold on," I said as he unzipped my jeans, and I twisted to reach for my phone on the table.

"Shall I smile for the camera? Are you going to take a shot of me undressing you?"

I cracked up as I scrolled through the music. "Count that as a never," I said, finding Matt Nathanson quickly and firing up a playlist. As the sexy pop music played, William grinned that devilish grin of his as he skimmed off my jeans.

"What?"

"Matt Nathanson," he said, shaking his head. "He's catnip for women."

"He is. But I'm going to let you in on a secret. You were getting lucky before I even turned him on."

"Excellent. Now I will continue turning you on," he said, and reached for my shirt, pulling it off me, then unhooked my bra, whistling low under his breath as my breasts tumbled free.

"I can't resist," he whispered, cupping my breasts and burying his face between them. Gasping loudly under his touch, my back bowed and I threaded my hands in his hair. I arched into him as he took his time lavishing attention, each sweet lick from his tongue sending a new round of desire crashing through my body. I closed my eyes, giving in to the moment, to the pleasure, to the intensity of his touch. He *was* catnip to me, and I was under some kind of spell, buzzed from the way he kissed and caressed, both tender and hungry. William made me feel wanted, and he made me want to let go for him, which was no easy feat for this control freak. I pulled him closer as he explored my flesh, sending hot sparks all through me. Soon he began inching his way down my body, trailing his tongue underneath the swell of my breasts to my belly. Then he licked an agonizingly sweet trail down my skin, past my belly button, and right to the top of my panties, where he flicked his tongue along the waistband and murmured, "These need to come off."

"They do," I moaned, tilting my hips to him. Gently, slowly, as if he was memorizing every single second of the undressing, he lowered my panties down my legs, moaning appreciatively when he saw me revealed to him for the first time. "Fuck, you're gorgeous, Jess," he said, and then tore them off the rest of the way. "I can't wait."

And then his lips were on me and I nearly screamed in pleasure. That first touch, that first moment when a guy kisses you there is the finest line in the sand—it's such a moment of sheer vulnerability. It's trusting him with your body, with yourself, with the chance to touch you in one of the most intimate ways. With him, I was bursting with longing, consumed by desire for him. And yet, lingering nerves nagged at the back of my mind, pricking me with the worry, the fear, and most of all, the hope that he wanted me the same way.

Not just my body, but my heart.

Because I wasn't just falling for him. I'd fallen. I was there on the other side, and I sure hoped he'd gone along for the ride, too.

Then I stopped worrying. Because the way he touched me, his lips savoring me like I was the most wonderful thing he'd ever tasted, not only settled all those nerves, but banished them far, far away. Nothing else mattered now, nothing but the here and now, the present with him, as he cupped my butt, angling me closer, flicking his tongue and pressing his lips against me. *Kissing me.* I gasped and moaned. Hell, I thrashed and cried out. Then I grabbed his hair, gripped his skull, and held on tight as he drove me to such a wondrous place that I was seeing stars. The whole world around me was silver and gold and pure epic pleasure as I shouted his name and exploded into thousands of brilliant pieces.

Minutes later, when the waves of pleasure started to ebb, and some semblance of logic returned to my brain, all I could think was I never knew anything could feel so good. I never knew anything could feel that intense. Now I knew, because what he'd done to me was beauty and bliss all at once.

He climbed on top of me, still fully clothed, and kissed my cheek, then my neck, and then he started to speak, but I cut him off.

"You know I have no clue what you're saying, right? I haven't had a magical Italian translation machine inserted in my brain to understand you in the bedroom."

He laughed, then pushed back on his arms to meet my eyes. The look in his eyes was one of satisfaction, but also something else entirely. Something I could almost pinpoint, but was afraid to.

"I wasn't going to speak in Italian. I was going to speak in English to tell you how much I loved doing that to you."

I couldn't help but smile. "I loved it, too."

"And now I have to be inside you. I want you so fucking much, Jess," he said, his eyes even darker than usual.

I shivered from the intensity of his words, and he wrapped his arms around me. "Are you cold?"

I shook my head. "No. I'm happy."

A smile curved his lips. The biggest smile I'd ever seen. He stood up, offered me his hand, and led me to my bedroom. He'd never been there before, but it wasn't hard to find in my small apartment.

"No movie posters?" he asked, arching an eyebrow as he scanned my walls.

"I'm a simple girl when it comes to decor."

The only picture on my wall was a framed shot of

the sun descending over the Pacific Ocean, rays of peach and dark pink streaking across the twilit sky.

He pointed to the image. "Did you take that?" he asked as I roamed my hands over his chest, feeling the outline of his muscles through his button-down shirt.

"Yes," I said, working my way down to his pants. "I do more than just celebrity shots. But those are the pictures I take just for fun."

"I never knew," he said. "It's beautiful."

"So are you in these wedding clothes, but I'd kind of like to get them off."

He returned his focus to me. "I can't think of anything I'd rather do than be naked with you," he said, and together we unbuttoned his shirt, and I pushed it off. Trailing my hands down his chest, I watched him as his eyes floated closed and he breathed out hard.

"*Jess.*"

"Yes?"

"I love the way you touch me," he said, and his voice was huskier than usual. It was his sex voice, I was learning. It was the way he sounded when we were alone, and I loved it.

"Good. Because it's one of my favorite things to do," I said, moving to the waistband of his pants. He kicked off his dress shoes as I unzipped his pants and pulled them down.

Clad only in boxer briefs that revealed exactly how turned on he was, he opened his eyes and pointed to his pants on the floor. "I should probably get a condom from those pants."

I laughed. "Yes. You absolutely should."

As he bent down to retrieve it from a pocket, I moved to my bed, stretching across the dark blue covers. He joined me, and I glanced down at his briefs, then my naked body. "There's an uneven distribution of clothing between us."

"Take them off," he said, and I could hear the desire in his voice.

I moved my hands to his waist, but then he stopped me, clasping his hand over mine. "Jess," he said, and this time the sexiness was gone—his voice was plain and full of need.

I pushed up on my elbows. "Are you okay?"

"Yes. So okay. So much more than okay. There's something I have to tell you."

And just like that, fear swooped through my body, expecting the worst, even though I had no clue what the worst would be. Except that somehow he'd used me.

15

William

The look in her eyes stunned me. They said she doubted me, and that only made me want to reassure her more. To tell her that everything between us was completely true.

Gripping her fingers tighter, I brought our clasped hands to my mouth and pressed a soft kiss to her knuckles. "I swear it's not bad. It's good. At least, I think it is," I said, then ran my other hand through her hair.

"Okay," she said softly, a tentativeness to her tone. She was waiting for me to go next, and that was perfectly understandable. I gulped, but that was only instinct telling me this was going to be hard to say. It wasn't hard to say. It was easy, like everything I felt for her.

"I just want to say this before we go any further," I began, keeping my gaze fixed on her. "And it's that I'm falling for you so much. It's way more than like. So much more. I'm falling in love with you, Jess."

She didn't say anything for a second, just exhaled. Then her lips parted, and she roped her arms around my neck. "I'm falling in love with you, too, William," she whispered, and my heart thumped hard against my chest, flooding with such happiness and hope. Knowing the girl you're crazy for is mad about you, too, is quite possibly the greatest feeling ever.

Well, there's only one other thing that comes close, and that was about to happen, too, since her fingers had found their way to my hand, and she was taking the condom from me.

"Please put this on now, and please make love to me," she said.

I pushed off my briefs, and obliged her request with a speed only race car drivers could rival. She opened her legs for me, and a bolt of heat tore through me. *Take it slow, Will,* I told myself. But fuck, I wanted her so badly that I didn't know if I'd be able to slow down. Settling between her legs, I entered her, stilling when I was all the way inside her. She felt so fucking good that my brain shut down, and my body took over.

So did hers as she wrapped her legs around me and moved with me, our bodies in perfect sync as if we were meant to fit together. Pleasure pulsed through me from the feel of her, so wet, so hot, and so fucking beautiful as she opened herself to me, her back bowing as I thrust deeper into her.

The sounds she made drove me on, not that I needed any help, mind you. But my focus was on her, and bringing her more pleasure, because the only thing that trumped how intense it felt being inside her for the first time was hearing her moans and noises, and the way they grew more frantic and fevered as I sank into her. I *loved* how much she let go when I touched her, how she gave herself to me with a kind of reckless abandon. Grabbing my hair, she pulled me close and whispered in my ear. "I love this. So much," she said, her breathing erratic, signaling that she was close.

"It's fucking fantastic being inside you, Jess. You feel so good to me," I told her, brushing an errant strand of hair away from her face. Keeping my eyes on her, I pushed deeper, reading her cues, giving her what her body was telling me she wanted. Her face contorted with pleasure, her eyes squeezing shut, her gorgeous lips falling open into a perfect O. Then a silent cry came first. She chased it with the loudest shout I'd ever heard, and it was music to my ears, because it was my name falling from her lips as she came. Seconds later, I was following her there, charging into a fantastic climax that was better than any other.

Because it was with her.

The girl that I'd fallen in love with.

My American girl.

* * *

We ordered a pizza later that night. The best part? She actually ate it. Well, she ate two slices.

"I can have this because we're going to work it off," she said.

"You have no idea how happy it makes me that you're not freaking out about food because of us," I said, gesturing from her to me.

She flashed me a smile. "Me, too. I was so sure I wouldn't be able to handle it all. But I'm thrilled to say I have no desire to barf because of falling for you," she said, bumping her shoulder against mine.

"Ah, I've never been so thrilled at not making a woman toss her cookies."

"I have a way with words, don't I?" she said, wiggling her eyebrows.

"You are blunt and it's adorable."

"Besides, as long as we keep working out like this, I don't think I'm going to have to worry about food one bit," she said.

A few minutes later, we christened her couch, and our second time was even better than our first as she climbed over me, riding me with a kind of wildness that made me lose my mind with pleasure.

Eventually, we returned to her bed where we tried several positions, laughing at the ones that didn't work so well, then not laughing at the ones that did.

Hell, we were both twenty-one. We had loads of energy. We had endless stamina. We had raging hormones, and we took advantage of all those points in our favor.

Jess

I stretched my arms over my head after my fourth orgasm of the night. It wasn't likely to be my last. William was insatiable, and that was fine with me. Sex with him rocked. It was so good it made me even more determined to help him find a job. I wasn't ready to give up this, or him.

"Hey, what time is your meeting tomorrow morning?"

"Nine."

"I have to meet Riley at eleven. Should we have coffee in between our meetings?" I asked, and I wasn't the slightest bit nervous about presuming we'd want to see each other as much as we could. I knew he wanted the same thing.

"You can't get enough of me," he said, grabbing my hip and pulling me close. "Now that you've had me, you're powerless to resist me."

"Well, duh," I said, rolling my eyes. "You're my Hot British Guy."

"The answer then is yes. On one condition."

"And that is?"

"You have to meet my brother. He's in town for work for the day, so we're getting together for brunch."

"I would love to meet him," I said, amazed at how

quickly we were falling into being a couple, especially when our clock was ticking. In less than two months, he might be gone, and the thought was a tight knot in my chest that I wanted to eradicate. For now, I turned my focus elsewhere, tapping the clock on my night-stand that blared ten thirty p.m. "The night is young. I'm going to expect several more rounds, William."

He saluted me. "Yes, ma'am. More sex coming your way, shortly." His gaze returned to the clock again. "Are those your flash cards next to the clock?"

Reaching for the stack of index cards, I nodded. "Yup. I practice before bed." I handed him the cards. "Try me."

"That's about twenty feet tall," he said as he held the huge mass of cards.

"A list to D list celebs," I said, and patted the cards. "C'mon. Quiz me. I can name everyone on here. I even added publicists the other night. They're on the top. Learned my lesson that I need to be able to recognize their faces."

He picked up the first card, and displayed the picture for me.

"Cassidy James," I said in less than a second. "She handles press for the cast of *Restless Roommates*, as well as for the actress Peach Winship from that LGO show *Powder* on drug dealers."

"Impressive," he said as he verified on the back, then showed me another one.

"Trivoli Lipton. He reps most of the *Stay-at-Home Moms with Sharp Claws* shows."

"Indeed he does," William said as he read the back

of the card.

He showed me another index card. "Lacey Cordona. Does PR for the *Smith Street Blues* series."

Then Keats's photo.

I laughed. "I think we both know who he reps."

"Yep. He reps jackasses," William said and I smiled at his remark.

He brandished a photo of another publicist, a smarmy-looking guy with a mane of wavy gray hair.

"That's Trevor Highsmith. British, as a matter of fact. Runs some big shop and reps a ton of writers and directors. I'm not positive but from a few stories I read, I think he might be Avery Brock's publicist."

William flipped the card around and looked at Trevor's photo. He furrowed his brow, as his expression shifted from amused to serious. "Are you sure?"

"Pretty sure. Why?"

William scratched his chin and studied the card. "He looks a bit like someone I know. But I'm not sure."

"Or maybe you just felt an instant kinship?" I offered. "Countryman and all."

"Right. That must be it," he said, then flashed a quick grin that didn't seem quite natural. He tucked the publicist cards in the middle of the stack, and returned them to the nightstand. "Let's talk about something besides publicists. Tell me more about your non-celebrity photography."

We spent the next few hours talking, and then exploring each other's bodies once again. There was no question it was the best night of my life.

SUNDAY

SUNDAY

Weather: 70 degrees, Sunny

16

<u>J</u>ess

William left my apartment shortly after the sun rose to shower and prep at his place for his meeting. Swatting away my temptation to sleep for another glorious hour, I forced myself out of bed so I could spend the morning studying before I saw him. After tackling biochemistry, I was ready to tackle William, so I showered, dressed, and rode over to the promenade, arriving five minutes early.

After I locked my scooter, I checked my phone and found a new text message from William.

Crap. My meeting is running late. Can you give me 30 min?

Like I was going to say no.

Besides, my good mood from falling in love had me walking on cloud nine, so I replied with a *yes*, then made my way to the nearest bookstore to see which shots my colleagues and competitors had landed in magazines last week. When I finished my perusal, I headed to the coffee shop, passing the brunch crowd at Rosanna's Hideout on the way. I scanned the tables on the deck in case I spotted a familiar face, and could whip off a few quick shots for J.P. to cheer him up. He was still sorely depressed over the wedding fiasco. I unzipped my backpack to reach for my camera, when I saw someone I knew.

Avery Brock.

With his publicist.

The smarmy-looking guy with the mane of wavy gray hair.

Avery was wearing shades, drinking a cup of coffee, and looking exceedingly irritated.

His publicist was drinking tea.

He was seated next to an older guy with a bald spot that was shiny in the morning sun.

There was a fourth person at the table, and that person wasn't drinking anything. That person was talking animatedly. That person was the person who'd made love to me less than twelve hours ago.

I blinked several times, trying to wish the tableau away. But every time, the players remained the same and so had the played—*me*. Because William fucking Harrigan was working for Avery fucking Brock.

All along. Throughout all our efforts. During the stakeout. As I passed him information. He was working for the scumbag, two-timing, cheating director and he never told me.

I burned.

No wonder William seemed fake when I showed him Trevor's flash card last night—the bastard knew him. Because the bastard was on his payroll, passing my intel onto the philandering toad.

Fire licked my insides, coating me in righteous anger. If William would lie about that, how on earth could I trust him about anything?

Every nerve ending in me snapped, every muscle in my body tightened, and every survival instinct from living in this town of liars and actors and fakers kicked in. Walking away was not an option. He needed to know I'd seen him. I left the camera safe and sound at the bottom of my backpack, and marched to the tables on the deck, claiming my post by the railing. This was our spectator sport in LA and it was one anyone could play—the spotted-someone-on-the-street game.

"Oh my God, William, is that you?" I said in my best over-the-top blond and bubbly California girl impression.

The guy I'd foolishly fallen in love with glanced at me, blinked twice, and swallowed hard. Like a deer in the headlights, he looked the same as when I marched up to him in Manhattan Beach and busted him for following me.

"I haven't seen you in, like, forever," I said, dragging out the last word. "How are you? How's school? How's your dog? You remember me, right? Claire Tinsley."

"Hi, Claire," he said in a strained voice.

"I have to tell you this story about a dog I was training. You gentlemen don't mind, do you?"

Avery said nothing. He crossed his arms, and slinked down further in the chair. The publicist affixed a fake smile that he probably flashed twenty-five times a day on his phony face. The guy with the bald spot grumbled *go ahead*.

"So I had this celebrity client—I can't say who he is, but I'm sure you understand, William, how important it is to not reveal who you work for," I said, giving him a sharp look as I went for the jugular with the reminder that he'd once said he could never tell me who his client was. "But his dog was being so naughty. His dog was literally humping all the lady dogs in the neighborhood."

The publicist cocked his head to the side. He seemed curious to hear my story now. William kept his face stony.

"And my client wanted to know how everyone else in the neighborhood kept taking all these pictures of his dog. How on earth could all the neighbors get shots of his pervy dog? As if it was the neighbors' fault that his dog was so randy. Can you believe that?" I said with an exaggerated huff. "I had to explain to him that the reason his dog kept getting caught on camera," I said, shifting my gaze to Avery Brock, "was that his dog was doing bad things." I let out a quick, fake laugh. "If he was a good boy, he'd never have to worry about getting caught with his pants down."

Then I waved toodle-oo and walked off down the promenade.

"Jess."

William called out to me thirty seconds later when I'd reached the corner of the street. I didn't turn around. I kept walking, seething inside. I would not give him the satisfaction. He had long legs, though, so he caught up to me, and placed a hand on my shoulder. "Jess," he said again. I shrugged off his hand, and turned to him. I took off my shades so he could see I wasn't crying. There was no room for tears.

"You were working for Avery Brock all along," I said pointing my finger sharply at him. "Your client was Avery Brock and you pretended you didn't know it. I told you everything and it went to that guy who you claimed was a dick, who you claimed was giving your countrymen a bad name." My voice rose and wobbled.

"I didn't know it, Jess, I swear," he said, pressing his palms together as if he were praying. "I had literally no idea until last night when you showed me the flash cards and I recognized Trevor because he's the client. But Trevor never told me he was having me do intel on behalf of Avery. I never would have done any of that for Avery."

"You told me last night you were done with the job. One more meeting and you were done with the job. I guess you're not done with the job, are you? Because you're sitting there feeding him information. *From me*," I said, now poking myself in the chest.

"Jess, it's not what you think."

"If there was ever a tired, old movie line, it's that one," I said with a scoff.

"Listen to me, please. I don't want to have anything to do with him. You have to believe me."

I flashed back to Nick Ballast's reaction when I tried to apologize to him on Friday morning. I could learn a thing or two from actors. They ran this town. They knew what to do. I had to be more like them. I took out my imaginary bow for my make-believe violin and pretended to play it.

Then I put my fake instrument away. "Actually, I don't have to believe you. Because there's this thing called honesty, William. I might be a control freak, I might be skeptical, I might be neurotic. But I never lied to you. Never," I said, biting out that last word. "I never lied about a thing. And you have lied about *so many* things," I said, and my voice started shaking. Fighting back, I reined in the tears that were threatening to flood my eyes. "And you always have an excuse or a reason why it's okay. But it's not. Especially because I *was* in love with you."

He exhaled heavily, his faced looked pinched. "*Was?*"

I was about to repeat myself when William's eyes danced away from me. "Oh bloody hell," he muttered, then waved listlessly. "Hi, Matthew."

From behind me, I heard footsteps, and I spun around, nearly smacking into William's ridiculously good-looking older brother. He had the same dark hair, the same chiseled cheekbones, the same fantastic smile—the only difference was Matthew had blue eyes.

"You must be Jess," he said to me with a big

grin, then offered a hand to shake. He had no clue we'd been arguing. "I've been looking forward to meeting you. I couldn't be more thrilled that this troublemaker has somehow convinced you he's a good guy."

William cringed, his jaw falling open. He shook his head at his brother, and made a slicing motion at his throat.

"What?" Matthew said, looking at William, then me, then back again. "Shit, did I say something wrong?"

I jumped in. "I assure you, it was nothing *you* said, and while I'd truly love to chat, my brunch meeting was just moved up. Sorry I have to duck out," I said, then I walked off without saying goodbye to William.

William

Matthew apologized profusely. Endlessly.

"I'm so sorry. I had no idea I was going to say the absolute wrong thing. I feel terrible," my brother said once more.

I shook my head, giving him utter absolution because everything was my fault. "Trust me. It's not you. It's me. It's all the things I didn't say. Or should have said at different times," I said, shoving a hand through my hair, then gesturing in the direction of the girl whose silhouette was fading in the distance. Like last night when I saw the flash card. When I realized who Trevor Highsmith was—that's when I should have said something.

"I should go after her," I said, and in a nanosecond, Matthew's palm was flat on my chest.

"No," he said crisply.

"No? Why?"

"Because when a woman walks away that pissed, you shouldn't follow her. She needs breathing space, and she *only* needs to see you again when you have a big fat fucking apology properly planned. Send her a text, tell her you're sorry and you love her, and then give her some room."

I narrowed my eyes at him. "I suppose that means you pissed off Jane at some point?"

He nodded several times. "I did. And take it from the voice of experience, the next thing we need to do is sit down, have a cup, and plan that proper apology. Assuming you still feel the same about her?"

I rolled my eyes. "Seriously? Do you have to ask?"

He held up his hands in surrender.

"Hey kid, what the hell?"

James's gruff, aggressive voice landed like wet concrete on my ears. Then I felt his clammy paw on my shoulder. "You don't just walk out when we're talking to a client. You get back in there and finish the hell up. That's how we do it in America," he said, digging his fingers into me.

Shrugging him off in one quick move, I swiveled around. For months, I'd been scratching and clawing at his door, hanging onto the frayed ends of his broken promises. Because I was desperate. Now I was done. I let go of that tattered rope, and let myself free fall, damn the consequences.

"Actually, James," I began, my tone even and measured. "I don't have to do anything of the sort. I don't have to talk to your client, or to Avery Brock, because I quit," I said and the words tasted like a victory prize. Even if I'd have nothing to show at the end of the day, being the first to leave was a vindication, and it was one I wanted more of. "Because that's how we do it in America. When someone strings us along, and toys with our future, and plays games, we don't have to take it. Thank you for all you've done, and no thanks to the letter of recommendation."

He huffed and puffed, fumes wafting out of his nostrils. "You can't do that."

I nodded and smiled at him. "Oh, I can, and I did, and I'm not done. Watch this," I said, then marched up to Avery Brock, parking my elbows on the railing and exhaling a *tsk tsk tsk*. "Avery, let me make this really simple for you," I said to the two-timing bastard. "Your publicist hired a security firm to find out why the paparazzi keeps getting so many pictures of you with your pants down. The answer is precisely what my friend Claire Tinsley said, but allow me to spell it out even more directly for you. You've been caught on camera because you're an ass. Because you cheat on your wife. Because you're doing something wrong. Here's the way not to get caught—*don't cheat*. Easy as pie. Good luck in your directorial endeavors, and may these latest foibles be a reminder to keep your dick in your pants."

A hand clamped down on my shoulder and jerked me away, possibly dislodging a shoulder blade in the process, though I couldn't be entirely certain. James's coffee-scented breath painted my cheek as he growled in my ear, "Leave the client alone, and get the hell out of here."

"No, Uncle James. You leave my brother the hell alone," Matthew said, interjecting as he grabbed me and steered me away from the bastard.

17

Jess

I did my best to pretend I wasn't in the foulest of moods. My effort was aided by the staff at the restaurant because I was treated like royalty when I gave the maître d' the name of the party, Ms. McDoodle, as Riley had instructed me. He escorted me to the best table in the restaurant and offered juice, tea, espresso, coconut water, or ginger soda, calorie-free of course, all compliments of the restaurant. I opted for a coffee.

A few minutes later, Riley arrived with Sparky McDoodle in her arms. Though the place was stuffed with other familiar faces, a noticeable buzz filled the air when Riley walked in and it wasn't simply because the restaurant had skirted all health code rules by allowing entry to a dog. She was such a rising star, no one could take their eyes off her. Riley waved to me, then flashed a big smile to a well-dressed man in a crisp white shirt and a yellow tie at a nearby table. He was seated next to a gorgeous redhead, who looked like she could be an actress, but since she was actually enjoying her food, I knew she wasn't. Riley held up her index finger to me, the sign she'd be right over, then stopped to give the man a quick hug. Next, she threw her arms around the woman. After the three of them chatted for a few seconds, Riley joined me.

"That was my new lawyer, Clay, and his wife, Julia. I hired him when I started my own production company. He's the best—he's all no-nonsense and works like hell to get me everything I could want in a deal," Riley said, breezily, as she sat down. Sparky McDoodle stayed in her lap, but thumped his tail at me.

"Look! He remembers that you saved his life," she said, beaming at her little pet as she stroked him between the ears. Unable to resist joining in the Sparky love, I reached over and scratched him on the chin.

"It is so good to see you," Riley said. "How are you, Jess?"

"Great," I said, but I don't think I was very convincing because Riley pushed her red sunglasses on top of her thick brown hair and asked me pointedly. "Really? You don't sound great. You sound like you're acting."

I managed a small laugh. "I guess I'm not a good actress."

"It's okay. I like it when people don't act. What's wrong?"

"I kind of had a crummy morning," I admitted, then reined in the truth, as I waved a hand in the air to dismiss the too-honest remark. "But don't worry about it. How are you? How was the wedding?"

"Amazing," she said, emphasizing every syllable. "It was so fun, and so silly, and I just got back from Vegas two hours ago, but it was exactly what my sister wanted. Only family, and we had a blast, and went to see one of those really cheesy over-the-top cabarets with showgirls and feathers, and we played poker, and she took off for Tahiti with Bradley this morning." She clapped her hand over her mouth. Then when she removed her hand, she whispered, "Oh, I'm not supposed to say that. Pretend you don't know she's in Tahiti."

I placed my fingers on my head as if they were brain suckers removing the information. "Gone. Removed. I totally forgot."

She laughed, and then we both ordered very little food, and after the waiter left, Riley leaned forward and said, "I wish I could do that to totally forget the script to *The Weekenders*. It starts shooting in a week, and like I told you, it's a wretched mess. The run-through Friday was a disaster," she said, picking up the thread of our phone chat about the movie.

"The script's really that bad?"

"It's awful. The director changed everything from the original. He doesn't have a clue what he's doing," Riley said, and she didn't sound fond of Avery, nor did she seem as if she was talking about a man she was canoodling with on the side.

"What's he like?" I asked carefully because I was treading on unfamiliar ground. I wasn't entirely sure of my own motives for asking—angling for info, or having a casual conversation with my dining companion.

"He's a total dick," she said, the disdain thick in her voice, and shocking me.

She seemed so into him the other night.

Seemed.

And that's when I started putting two and two together. Known for his speedy exits, Avery must have already dumped Riley, and now she was ticked at him because she'd been the one spurned. Glancing furtively from side to side, as if she were scanning for spies, she leaned even closer and whispered, "He broke my best friend's heart."

Or maybe not. Because the plot was thickening, and now I didn't question my own motives because they were simple—I was damn curious for curiosity's sake.

"Who's that?"

"Andy Blue," she mouthed, referring to Andromeda Blue, one of the other young actresses on Avery's list of prior conquests.

"Was she in love with him or something?"

"Completely."

As I opened my mouth to ask how on earth Riley could be fooling around with him when he'd broken her best friend's heart, I stopped myself before I said a word—I couldn't let on that I knew Riley was involved with him. That information wasn't public knowledge, so I said nothing.

"And because of that, I would so love to take him down," she added.

I laughed once, because that desire—to take someone down—seemed to be going around. "You want to get him off the picture?" I joked, returning the conversation to *The Weekenders*.

But she didn't laugh. She seemed intensely serious as she nodded several times. "He has a no-cheating clause. If he's caught cheating again, the studio boots him."

"I've never heard of a studio doing that."

"The studio didn't do it," she said, continuing in her I'm-sharing-a-secret-whisper. "His wife did. She made sure it was in his contract. But enough about this sordid business. Tell me more about you."

The cogs in my brain were already turning, and I rewound to the day I first learned from Keats about the Avery-Riley pairing. My initial instinct had been that Riley was too smart to get involved with her director. Had my instinct been right after all? Because something else was going on behind the scenes. The real story was playing out while no one thought anyone was watching. And the real story was something else entirely—it was subterfuge, it was revenge on behalf of the best friend, it was everyone-has-an-agenda.

But her agenda right now was of the getting-to-know-you kind.

"Where do you go to school?" Riley continued, and she sounded truly interested in me. Even though I'd vowed not to be seduced by actors again, the fact was she was good. Whether she was playing or not, I wanted to tell her the truth. Because I wasn't an actor. I wasn't a player. I was no good at pretending, and I didn't want to fake my way through this meal with Riley any longer.

Besides, I had nothing to lose. And if I'd learned anything from my week with William it was that any relationship—even one that promised to be as brief as this moment in time with Riley—ought to be based on honesty.

"I'm pre-med at the University of Los Angeles. I graduate in two months, and then I'm going to med school, and I pay my way through school by taking pictures of celebrities," I said in as business-like a tone as I could manage.

As if I hadn't just dropped the worst bombshell possible into a celebrity's lap. *Hello, you're having lunch with a paparazzo! Sucker!*

Riley's eyes widened, and she clutched Sparky McDoodle to her chest. His ears perked up, and he looked sharply at me, too, as if he was admonishing me.

"You do?" she asked, raising an eyebrow.

"Yeah, I do," I said matter of factly. "That's why I was there that day in Manhattan Beach. I was there to take your picture at the bridesmaid fitting. Or fake bridesmaid fitting, I should say. Only I never got the picture because of what happened with Sparky

McDoodle. And I also tried to crash your sister's wedding yesterday, only I wound up crashing the fake wedding down in Ojai Ranch and I got some great photos of all the actors hired as stand-ins for guests, and even the actress they hired for you," I said, and I leaned back in my chair, feeling in control as I unspooled the very true story of my life.

She listened with her mouth agape as I told the tale of the moment when her sister's doppelgänger walked down the aisle. Her big brown eyes widened to planet-size, and she motioned with her fingers for me to tell her more. Oh, did I ever have more to tell. I had the goods, and I went for broke, laying it all out. "But I have real pictures of you, too, because Jenner Davies hired me through his publicist's younger brother to take pictures of you and Avery making out outside the smog facility in Burbank the other night, and Jenner used them to bribe Avery to get Nick's role in *The Weekenders*. But supposedly, and I have no idea if this is true because it came from a guy who pretended to like me but was really playing me, Nick wanted off the movie to go do a TV show, so both Nick and Jenner were in on the blackmail scheme. Oh, there's one more thing. I got your right side when I took the pictures."

There it was. The whole damn story.

Riley's mouth turned into a giant O. She didn't speak. She sat there in shock that might have morphed into admiration, because soon she was grinning. "You got my right side?" she said, as amazed as if I had just told her I'd stolen a Van Gogh and fenced it for millions.

I nodded.

"Do you have them still? The pictures?"

"I do. I may even have them on my phone. Want to see them?"

"Yes," she said, and I found it odd that she wasn't walking away, or throwing a fit, or tossing ice-cold water on me. But that could still come. Even so, I reached into my back pocket for my phone. I'd put it on silent, and I had missed a few calls, but I didn't look at the missed call list. Quickly locating one of the shots, I held my phone out to show her, careful to keep a tight grip on it.

She shook her head in appreciation. "That is a great picture," she declared, tapping a finger on the screen. "And do you know what this means?"

"What does it mean?" I asked, figuring this would be the moment when she went full actress on me, drama queen and all. Tablecloth yanked, drink tossed in my face, the works.

Instead, she raised one eyebrow, then rested her chin in her hands, the most delighted look spreading across her face. "It means I don't have to get together with that toad again to take him down. I don't have to kiss him again. I was going to let it slip to the media that we were hooking up tonight. I didn't say anything the first night because I didn't know how it would go. But I was going to drop a hint to the press before tonight, so that the girl who took the shots of my sister's wedding could get pictures of him and me. Then I could get him off the movie because of his no-cheating clause. But I don't have to now," she said, with wide eyes and a massive smile, as if I've just presented her with the greatest gift in the world. Then she turned serious. "That is, if you'll let me leak these photos."

My head spun, and my jaw dropped. Talk about a turn of events. Even as the shock coursed through my veins, my natural skepticism quickly returned. "But aren't you annoyed that I'm a paparazzo?"

"Let's see," Riley said, lifting her perfectly mani-cured hands and counting off on each finger as she spoke. "You snapped pictures of my good side when I had to face-lock with that scum. You never once asked for details of my sister's wedding when we were on the phone and you easily could have used me for informa-tion. And the first time we sat down and talked for more than two minutes, you told me exactly who you were and why. Not to mention the most important thing. You saved my dog's life. In case it's not clear, this dog," she said, stopping to pet the pampered pooch again, "is the love of my life, and you made sure he's still in my life. So, no. I'm not annoyed. In fact, I'm dying to hear more."

William

A little later, we were drinking tea, like proper English

men on a Sunday morning, and hatching a plan to get the girl back.

"What does she love? I mean, besides the second most handsome Harrigan brother?" Matthew asked as he leaned back in his chair, crossed his legs, and took a drink of his English breakfast tea.

"Movies. She's completely besotted with Hollywood."

Matthew dipped his hand into the back pocket of his jeans, and grabbed a small notebook. "Let's be scientific and write this down," he said, then opened it to a random page and jotted down in his blocky handwriting *films*.

"Dogs," I added, thinking of Jennifer and the pet therapy work Jess did with her at the hospital. I quickly told Matthew about her volunteer gig.

"She's a keeper. Seriously. Smart, kind, hot, loves dogs, and somehow she can tolerate you," Matthew said, then flashed me a quick grin. "See, I can mock you now since it's only you and me."

"Mock away. But if this doesn't work, I reserve the right to knock you one on the chin."

"Okay, what else?" he asked, flipping to another page. Then he pointed to a few names written on the opposite page in the notebook. "I don't want to write on the backside of that page. That's the name and number of the publicist I'm meeting who set up the interview with the band I'm here to see."

I snapped my fingers. "Publicists!"

"Publicists?"

"That's another thing she loves."

"Publicists?" he repeated, incredulous.

"Let me explain," I said, and rewound to the flash cards that started this whole fiasco.

When I was finished, Matthew eyed his notebook knowingly, then waved it in front of me. "I have the answer."

18

Jess

As our food arrived, I told her everything, like she'd asked for. I shared the story of how I became a celebrity photographer, how I worked the pedicure patrol and shopping beats regularly, how we'd gotten the tip about her and Miles last week, and how that shot had led Keats to call me for his phony photo agency. I told her about William as well, and how he turned out to be working for Avery Brock.

"Miles is such a sweetie," she said, twirling a strand of her hair.

"Are you going out with him?"

"Oh no," she said, shaking her head. "Miles and I are just friends. I would never have kissed Avery, even though I was faking it, if I was with someone. And now, you and I are going to take Avery down, right?"

Riley said, as if the two of us were now in cahoots in the ultimate heist.

"Sure," I said with a weirdly happy shrug. I wasn't happy about William. But I was happy—in some way—to talk to Riley and tell her the whole truth. "He deserves it."

Riley twirled a strand of her hair. "You know, Jess, I've been looking for a great story for my production company."

"Yeah?"

"This is a great story. This would make a great movie."

"You think so?" I asked as I took a sip of my water, eyeing her over the top of the glass.

She narrowed her eyes, held out her hands as if she were framing a shot. "I can see it now. *My Life as a Teen Paparazzo.*"

"Not a bad title. Even though I'm twenty-one."

"I know. But in the film we'll make you eighteen. I'm serious. I want to buy your story. For my production company."

"Really?" I said with a scoff. I didn't believe her, because this simply wasn't believable. Not in my world where my *tuition due* dreams had been foiled by a sea of extras under a rented tent.

But the next thing I knew, Riley was waving to her lawyer across the restaurant.

"Give me one second," she said, then scurried over to his table, Sparky McDoodle snug in her arms, and chatted briefly with him. Then he and his wife stood up, left their napkins on their chairs, and joined us at our table. In a heartbeat, a waiter appeared with chairs for them. It was good to be Hollywood royalty.

Riley introduced me to her lawyer and his wife, and I shook hands with both of them, then waited to see what was up her sleeve.

"Clay, do you and your fabulous wife have two seconds to hear a pitch for my production company?" Riley asked.

"Of course," he said, in a deep, gravelly voice, and if he weren't a lawyer, he'd make a hell of a voice-over actor. Come to think of it, he'd be pretty damn fine on camera, too, since he had the tall, dark, and handsome look down pat. His wife, all curves and confident beauty, was a perfect match.

"Lay it on us," she chimed in, and he gripped her hand and smiled briefly at her. I felt a momentary pang of missing—these two seemed like such a team, and I had felt that with William. But I had to brush away the thoughts of him.

Riley began by holding up her hands and spreading them slowly, the universal sign language in Hollywood signaling the start of a pitch. "*My Life as a Teen Paparazzo.* Celebrity photographer and senior in high school—we'll call her Tess in the script— becomes involved in a plot to take down a director who can't keep his hands to himself. Everyone has an agenda and everyone is trying to give someone else the screw, except for our fearless heroine who's simply trying to pay for medical school. Along the way she has to team up with a hotshot young private eye to try to crash the wedding of the century, but in the end he's working for the director. She wonders if she can ever trust him again?"

She held out her hands in a what-more-could-I-want gesture. "What do you think?" she asked, directing her question to Clay. "Should I do it for McDoodles Productions?"

"Riley, you should work on the projects that make you happy," he said, keeping his eyes fixed on his client the whole time. "That's my best advice to you as a person. As your lawyer, it sounds like the kind of project that you would love, which means it sounds like you could turn it into a big hit."

"I'd go see that movie, and I'm not just saying that because my husband's client is behind it," his wife said.

"What do you think?" Riley asked, and I wasn't sure who she was speaking to at first. Then I noticed she was looking down. At her lap. Asking her dog. "Do you think it's a good idea?" She lowered her ear to the dog, pretending to listen to him. When she raised her head, she said, "Sparky McDoodle agrees, so it's settled. Clay, can you draw up a deal memo tomorrow and get it to my friend Jess? It's her life story, and I'm buying the rights, and I'm playing her."

Riley tossed around some figures, and they all sounded marvelous to me, but then again, numbers in the high five-figures with dollar signs attached to them had a way of sounding marvelous to me. Even so, I wasn't going to fall in love with the possibility of a big payday again. I didn't know if Riley meant any of this. I didn't know if I'd ever hear from her again. I'd believe it when and if it happened, because I've seen enough of this town to know that a deal isn't done until it's signed, sealed, and delivered, and even then the terms could change.

I couldn't let myself get wrapped up in the prospect of winning the lottery, when the lottery could just as easily go bust. I'd saved enough already for a few classes, as Anaka had said, and if I had to keep taking pictures of pedicures and parking tickets to pay for another year and then another, I'd do that. I'd layer in my occasional shoots with Jillian when she needed a local photographer for the football team. If I had to find a loan, then I'd go that route. I knew who I was, and I knew who I would be. I wasn't the star, I wasn't an actor, I was simply a paparazzo who wanted to be a doctor, and who had to pay her own way through Hollywood. That was fine by me.

"I'll get you the deal memo in the morning," Clay said as his wife stroked the little dog's tan chin. He lifted his tiny snout closer to her hand, savoring the attention.

"Is Sparky McDoodle going to play himself?" Julia asked, and it was endearing how everyone treated the dog as if he were a vital cog in the Riley machinery, because, of course, he was. Sparky McDoodle made this actress tick. He was her one true thing, the creature in her life whose reactions she could trust completely, I suspected.

Riley shook her head and covered the dog's ears. "I want him to grow up and have a normal life. I don't want him to feel the pressure of show biz. There's only one thing, though," Riley said to me and I figured this would be the moment when she told me it was all a joke. That once again, I'd been played. "We need a happy ending," she said to me.

I furrowed my brow. "What do you mean? The actress and the photog take down the director. That's the happy ending," I said as if it were obvious. Because, well, wasn't it?

"No," Riley said, as if she had a secret up her sleeve. "That's the ending of a girl-power buddy flick. This movie is going to be a romantic comedy mystery with a twisty, turny plot. It's going to be about the clever photog and the gorgeous private eye, and how they fall for each other while trying to crash a celebrity wedding. We need a happy ending with the guy."

"But there is no happy ending with the guy," I said in a firm voice. After all, William was working for the bad guy. How could there be a happy ending?

Riley sighed. "Jess, call me crazy. But I just have a feeling this guy really was doing what he said he was doing this morning. I don't know why. But I believe it in my heart. I believe this is the part where the girl thinks the boy screwed her over, but he really didn't, so she needs to make up with him."

Julia nodded, flashing a gorgeous smile. "That's your happy ending." Then she shifted closer to me, and dropped her hand on top of mine. "And listen, sometimes men just do dumbass things. They don't think. Or if they do, they think they're doing some-thing for your best interests. And in the end, you give him a chance to explain and then you forgive him. So long as he's the real deal," she said, and the last few words were directed to her husband, who looked at her with such a combination of adoration and lust that I'd never seen before.

Except…maybe…when William looked at me?

I weighed my options as I replayed the last seven days with William. On the one hand, I could conclude that every moment had been a smooth and well-orchestrated ruse. Or I could go with my gut. When I was with him I didn't feel all work and no play. I felt carefree and light-hearted. I felt wanted and desired. I felt fun and happy. And I felt all those things without spiraling back into my bad habits. William was ice cream and French fries without the guilt. He was something I'd denied myself for years. Something I wanted again.

And just like that, the movie montage began, reel after reel of our times together playing before my eyes. Our first kiss when I surprised him on the boardwalk. His text that night: *How do I move that maybe to a yes?* The things he said to me in Italian when we made out on his motorcycle. The kiss outside the hospital, the Busy Bee Eatery when I fed him a pineapple, the dinner he made me and how it was exactly what I wanted to eat. Then the couch, oh the couch, the things we did on the couch. The rollercoaster, and after the rollercoaster, and then yesterday at my apartment. My insides melted from the memories, and if I let myself linger on yesterday—yesterday evening to be precise—I was going to start squirming in this chair and then rocket on out of this restaurant on lust alone.

And love. Because damn it. I *was* in love with him. Present tense. Future tense. All tenses. In every single way. And I hoped to hell he had a reasonable explanation. Somewhere inside, I knew he did. Because I trusted myself and I wouldn't have felt the way I did for him if he was a jerk. I had to give him the benefit of the doubt, and give him a chance to explain.

I could believe everyone in Hollywood was a bastard. Or I could believe that only some people in Hollywood were, and that the rest were just people. Besides, the one thing I knew to be a cold, hard fact of the movies and of life was this—when someone gives you a chance for a happy ending, you don't leave the audience hanging. You give them what they want, and what the audience wants often has a funny way of being exactly what you want, too.

"I bet he's been trying to call you and explain," Riley said softly.

"Maybe he has," I said in a small voice, hoping she was right as I took out my phone again and scrolled through my text messages.

HBG: I'm sorry. Please let me explain, but I also want to say I was never playing you. I'm not working for James or Avery anymore, and I told them both exactly what I think of them. And I'm not just falling in love with you. I'm madly in love with you. Let's be mad together. Can we get to the part in the script where we make up?

I didn't even try to contain the wild smile curving up my lips.

"I told you so," Riley said as if she'd just won a bet. "He said it was all a misunderstanding, right?"

"Sort of," I said, then lifted my face from the phone. The three of them were all grinning knowingly, and even though I rarely let people in, even though I kept a distance most of the time, I was with kindred spirits. Movie lovers. Lovers of a happy ending. I sensed it from spending the tiniest bit of time with Julia and Clay, and I knew it innately from my moments with Riley. Setting my phone aside, I laced my fingers together. "I think I need to do that thing at the end of the movies where they run to the airport, stop the plane, clear up the misunderstanding kind of thing."

"Yes, you do," Riley said, and she and her lawyer and his wife waved me off.

19

William

My phone stared at me from the center of the table as Matthew paid the bill. The screen seemed dreadfully naked without her name popping up in reply to my text. I had a sinking feeling Jess was masterful at the silent treatment. Not because she was cold or cruel, but because she was focused and determined, and if she wanted to keep me out of her life for good, she'd do so. That same steeliness that drove her to excel in school and work surely was going to bite me in the ass, because it would give her the fuel to blow me off. For good.

But she was right—I should have told her Trevor was the client when I saw his face on the flash cards. I simply hadn't known who Trevor was repping. Perhaps he'd told James, and James knew he was sending me hunting for intel for Avery Brock, but then James had a way of never disclosing the details, so I'd never known I was fishing for Avery.

Matthew pushed back in his chair. "I should hit the road and head over to my interview. Remind me now, I drive on the left side of the road here, correct?" he said, teasing.

"You've been in this country for ten years," I said. "Right side, man. Right side."

"And I have the pleasure of living in New York City, which means I rarely have to drive."

"Why don't you just try the left side then and see how well that works out for you," I suggested as we weaved through the tables on our way out of the restaurant where coffee had turned into eggs, potatoes, and pancakes. Matthew was a lot like me—we liked our food, and we liked to exercise and work it off.

Outside the restaurant, he dropped his shades over his eyes, and I did the same. It was a typical Los Angeles day, sunny and seventy degrees without a cloud in the sky. A pang of longing scratched through my veins—I would miss this town.

"I really need to find a job," I said, stating the obvious.

Matthew clapped me on the back. "There's time, Will. We've got two months. Do you have any more interviews lined up?"

"I'm going to reconnect with a few of the employment agencies this week," I said.

"We'll keep talking. We'll keep brainstorming, and we'll figure something out," he said, then gave me a brief brotherly hug. "For now, you are a man on a mission. Get your woman back. I expect a full report tonight on how successful our plan was."

I arched an eyebrow. "Full report? If we're successful, I'll be too busy for that."

He shook his head, laughing. "Let me amend that. All I want is a modified report that you won her heart. The rest of the details, please keep to yourself."

Then he said goodbye, and I walked the two blocks to my bike, strapped on a helmet, and revved the engine. Just as I was about to take off, I felt a buzzing in my back pocket. A flicker of hope ignited in me. *Please let it be her.*

When I saw her name flashing on my screen, that flicker turned into a full flame. "Hey," I said when I answered.

"Hi. Are you at home?"

"No, but I'm on my way. Why?"

"Can I meet you there in an hour and twenty-five minutes?" she asked, but her voice gave nothing away. Even so, the fact that she wanted to meet in person gave me hope that I was out of the doghouse.

"That's a rather precise time," I said with a laugh.

Rewarded with a small chuckle in response, my heart lightened more. I'd won her over in the first place with laughter; I wanted to keep her with it, and everything else, too. "Yes. Timing matters," she said, then added in a softer voice. "I'll see you soon, William."

It was the way she said my name as she hung up that thrilled me the most. She said it like I was the only one who knew that softer side of her. With the wind at my back, I pulled onto the road, then darted in between cars on the way to my apartment. Time was ticking, and I had to finish a project for her. After a quick stop at the office supply store, I reached my building and dashed up the steps to my apartment, bumping into John on the landing for the second floor. His fist was raised in a knock on my door.

Rubbing my eyes as if the sight shocked me, I said, "Is it you, John? Or your twin brother, since you've never been known to request entry to my humble abode. You usually just enter."

He raised the plastic shopping bag he was holding. "And to think I was about to replenish the milk I drank. I think I'll keep it now."

"Did you bring me cereal, too? It goes well with milk," I said, as I unlocked the door and let him in. As the door fell shut, I swiped the bag from him, said thanks, and tucked the milk carton neatly on the shelf in the fridge.

"Funny how that slipped my mind," he said, scratching his chin. "But I'm happy to check your cupboards and finish off whatever cereal you have."

"Let's take a raincheck on that. I need to do something right now before Jess comes over."

He wiggled an eyebrow. "Be sure to leave a sock on the door. It's the only sure-fire way to guarantee I won't enter unannounced."

I shook my head and laughed. "Good to know that socks, not locks, are where you draw the line at breaking and entering."

"It's not breaking in when you don't lock it. Anyway, you up for volleyball tomorrow?"

"Would love to. But I need to get some stuff done first. Classes and the job hunt, you know."

"Good luck, man," he said and knocked his fist against mine before he left.

Then I emptied the contents of the bag from the office supply store and set to work.

Jess

The toothpick revealed that nirvana had been achieved. There was nothing on it, so I grabbed an oven mitt, then removed the pan and placed it on a cooling rack.

"Smells divine," Anaka said, wafting the sweet scent of the creation into her nostrils.

"I'd give you some…but then I'd have to work you overtime as a screenwriter and make you come up with another suitable gift."

"I'd be more than willing to be used for those skills. But, for now, tell me more about last night while we wait for this to cool," she said, tugging me away from the kitchen and to the couch.

"Speaking of last night, we had a nice time on the couch," I said, patting the cushion.

She grabbed my arm and yanked me up, then pulled me over to the table. "There better be a new couch delivered here by tomorrow," she said, wagging her finger at me.

"Duly noted."

"Now. Details. I want them."

As I shared bits and pieces of last night, my skin grew warm all over. But it wasn't from the memories —oh so potent—of our physical connection. It was from telling the story of what he said, and the way he said it, and how we talked to each other. Like friends. Sure, I kissed him the first day I met him, and I kissed him so many times after that. But we became friends. And then we became more. Telling the story of how we said we were falling in love was like experiencing it all over again, and telling it reminded me, too, to trust the guy I was in love with. I'd trusted him with my heart, and I had to trust he had his reasons.

Whatever they were, the bottom line remained the same. No matter what, no matter how, I was going to find a way for him to stay.

20

William

Exactly one hour and twenty-five minutes after her call, I heard the most beautiful sound in the world. A knock on my door. For the briefest of moments, it occurred to me that John might be popping back over. But when I opened the door, it was Jess. She was wearing a short skirt and she was holding a cake.

It smelled delicious.

"I can bake," she said, sounding like the girl I fell for. Confident. Brazen. Certain of herself.

"I see. Or rather, I smell. Smells good."

"It's chocolate cake."

"I like chocolate cake."

"I know. You told me the day I met you. And you told me again the day you asked me to go to the wedding," she said, still standing in my door. Looking hot and edible and *here*. I quickly reached behind her and shut the door. Then I locked it, since that was classier than putting a sock on it and would serve the same purpose.

"And you told me, too, I was like cake, which I knew was high praise from you," I said, keeping my hands at my sides. My fingers itched to touch her, but I hadn't been given permission again yet.

"It *was*," she said, emphasizing that verb as she kept her eyes locked on me. "And it still *is*. And this cake is my way of saying I'm sorry I walked off this morning. You don't have to explain because I'm choosing to trust that you aren't the type of guy who would ever knowingly work for Avery Brock. And you're not the type of guy who would ever willfully deceive me. I'm choosing to believe you're still the same guy I fell in love with," she said, and my heart damn nearly soared out of my chest.

"I am. I am that guy. I swear," I said, never looking away from her. Never wanting to lose touch with those beautiful blue eyes, so pure and true. "I should have said something when I saw Trevor's picture, but I wanted to focus on you, and us. Being with you was so damn amazing that I didn't want to ruin it by bringing those pigs into our night together. But you have to believe me—James never told me that Avery was the client. All I knew was we were working for Trevor's shop and that was all."

"I know," she said softly. "I believe you."

Her words were the sweetest song playing just for me. They were my catnip.

"When I sat down to the meeting this morning, I was still working out how to extract myself from Avery. Because I don't want to work for someone like that. Or for James. And I told them both off this morning. You would have loved it, actually."

"What did you say?" she asked, her natural curiosity plain as day in the sparkle in her eyes.

I shared every single detail of the moment by the railing and she nearly squealed in delight. "That is perfect," she said. "I wish I'd been there to see it."

"Me, too. But you're here now and that's all that matters."

"Well," she began, eyeing the cake pan in her hands. "There is something else that matters. This cake."

"Was it hard for you to make it?" I asked gently. "Did it tempt you?"

"Yes, and no. It was hard, but I managed it. Because I wanted to do it for you. Want to take off the tinfoil?"

"Yes." I peeled it back to discover a chocolate cake that looked absolutely mouth-watering. The best part was the writing on it. In orange lettering across the frosting, she'd written the word *Stay*. Then under it was a full sentence: *You are the top of my to-do list for the next two months.*

"I don't know if it's dirty or romantic, or both, but I'll take any and all from you. Let me put this cake down so I can kiss you," I said, taking the pan from her outstretched arms and setting it on the table. When I returned to her, she had the sweetest and sexiest look on her face.

"It was both," she said. "And it's a promise that I'll do everything I can to help you stay. When I set my mind on a goal, I'm really good at staying focused on it. You and your job hunt are going to be at the top of my to-do list."

Unable to resist touching her any longer, I threaded my fingers through her hair, loving the feel of it against my skin. "Being on your to-do list in any form is about the best thing I could ever ask for," I said.

"Can this be the part where the hero and heroine kiss and make up?"

I answered her with my lips, kissing her softly as she returned to me. Taking my time, I let the kiss linger as I sucked gently on her lower lip, thrilling at the small gasp that escaped her lips. I covered her mouth with mine, sliding my tongue against hers, and the taste of her was divine. Like sunshine and music, and so damn delicious that I didn't want to go slow anymore.

The kiss changed gears, picking up speed in a heartbeat, as I kissed her more deeply, crushing her to my chest, where she belonged, where I wanted her, and where I needed her. Jess had arrived in my life unexpectedly a mere seven days ago, but she was everything I could ever want—smart, funny, gorgeous, determined, and daring as hell. Soon her hands were in my hair, and she was pulling me even closer, her mouth fusing with mine as we kissed furiously. As if it had been too long since we touched each other. And for us, it had. We made up for the morning and the early afternoon apart with a kiss that made my mind foggy. My body was on high alert, and I was hungry for more of her. For all of her.

The kiss went on and on, and it could have lasted the whole afternoon for all I knew. I lost track of everything but the feel of her, the way she responded, the sweet little murmurs she made as we collided, mouths, lips, teeth, and tongue coming together.

Eventually, we came up for air, lips bruised from another epic kiss.

"It's never been like this before," she said, her voice breathy, her cheeks rosy.

"The way we kiss?"

"Yes," she said, her fingers brushing against my neck. "No one has ever kissed me the way you do, William."

There it was. My name on her lips, melting me again for her. "Good. I can't stand the thought of anyone else ever kissing you," I said, running my index finger across her lower lip. "And by the way, I'm still madly in love with you. And I just wanted to say that."

"Wait. Last night it was falling in love. Now it's been bumped up to madly in love?" she raised an eyebrow playfully.

"Can you fault me for falling this fast? I think you're amazing, so you only have yourself to blame for how quickly it happened. And now, I have something for you."

"For me?"

I rolled my eyes. "I'm madly in love with a girl who loves romantic comedies. You think I'm going to let you be the only one with a gift?"

A smile tugged up the corners of her lips as I grabbed the gift I'd left on the table. "I hope you'll forgive me for not wrapping it, but here it is," I said, handing her a stack of flash cards.

Her eyes sparkled with curiosity and wonder as she considered the first card. A photo of an auburn-haired woman wearing cat's eye glasses.

"Jasmine Spoonville," she said as she ran her finger over the photo I'd printed out, then she flipped the card, reading aloud the details. "Publicist for Dr. Jade. The rising hip-hop star." She slid it under the pile, moving onto the next one. "Chase Henry." The bleached-blond publicist with plugs in both ears flashed his teeth at Jess. "Reps Protracted Envy. I love their music. I read about their new album in *On the Surface* last week. LA's hottest band. This is like a treasure chest," she said as she held the stack tight against her chest.

I nodded. "I noticed you didn't have publicist cards for rock stars. Or even take photos of rock stars very often. And a ton of musicians are in LA, and my brother gave me intel on them. I thought this could be a way to expand your repertoire. I know it won't make up for the loss of the wedding shot, but it's a start, right?"

"It's a huge start," she said, throwing her arms around my neck, the cards still in her hands. "I never even thought about focusing on rock stars. Beyond the obvious ones. But this is incredible, and I love it. And you."

"Excellent. Now go put those cards down because I have other plans for you."

Jess

His plans involved hiking my skirt up to my hips and scooting me onto the kitchen table. One of his legs came between mine, and he used it to spread me open. Then he moved closer, tugging off my shirt and feathering his hands across the bare skin of my shoulders, arms, and then my waist. Mapping my body, like an intrepid explorer, eagerly discovering new lands, he roamed his hands up the soft skin of my belly and around to my back. I trembled from his touch, letting my head fall back as he found the clasp of my bra, unhooked it, and dropped it into a chair. Then he cupped my breasts and moaned appreciatively.

"If you ever can't find me, it's because I got lost touching your breasts," he said, as he ran his thumbs under, over, all around.

I laughed. "I think I'd know where to find you, if that's where you were."

"I could spend all day here," he said, lowering his head to my chest to plant kisses all across my flesh.

My laugh turned into a needy groan as he teased me with his tongue, then nipped me with his teeth. His soft hair brushed against my skin, a sweet reminder of all the ways he could touch me, all the sensations he brought to my body. I slid one hand to the back of his head, holding him against me. He flicked his tongue across me, continuing his slow, sensual torture. Heat spread like wildfire in my veins, and I ached with desire for him.

I couldn't take a slow tease right now. In the grand scheme of time, it hadn't been long since he'd made love to me. The blink of an eye, the tick of the second hand on the clock, but in the narrow span of my life, it felt like ages since I'd had him. And I desperately wanted him inside me. Wanted to be filled up by him. Wanted to feel his hard length slide inside of me, where I was hot and ready for him.

Now.

I opened my eyes, and gently tugged him up.

"I can't wait," I said. "Don't make me wait. Don't torture me right now."

"Torture will come another time," he said, reaching into his pocket for a condom as I pulled off his shirt and trailed my fingers across the firm planes of his chest and down to his perfectly chiseled abdomen. I unzipped his jeans, and pushed them to his knees as he rolled on the condom. Then he was rubbing against me as I spread my legs wider. He entered me slowly, my breath catching from the delicious feel of him exactly where I wanted him.

He whispered something in Italian, and I shook my head. "No. No more keeping me in the dark. I want to know what you said."

He started to sink into me, whispering hotly in my ear. "I want you so badly. I love being inside you. I love feeling you come on me."

My skin sizzled. I arched into him as he took his time entering me. My body was a neon sign begging for him, as the most thrilling sensations flooded from his dirty words. "I want you to teach me how to say that. I want to know naughty Italian, too, so I can say dirty things to you," I said, wriggling closer, trying to bring him deeper. Bring him all the way in.

"I will teach you," he said in a sexy growl as he buried himself in me.

Then we didn't need any more words, and I didn't think I could form them anyway.

He lowered his mouth to mine. As he brushed his lips against me, he started thrusting. Deep, hard, fast. The way I needed it right now, his kisses driving me as wild as the sheer bliss of him inside me did. He held my hips firmly in his hands, rocking into me, all while his soft, sweet lips claimed mine in yet another endlessly perfect kiss.

Kissing him was heaven. Making love to him was better than that—it was another land, bathed only in bliss, as I came apart in his arms.

Forget all the stars with their million dollar movies, their mansions, their fancy cars.

I was the luckiest girl in Hollywood.

* * *

Later that afternoon, we found ourselves in his bed.

With his laptop. Cruising Craigslist and all the job boards we could find, and coming up with plans for him.

We were a team again, and that's how we worked best.

21

One Week Later
Weather: 70 degrees, Sunny

<u>Jess</u>

I tapped open the article in *Hollywood Breakdown*, the premiere magazine for all of the insider Hollywood news. But not the kind I documented. There were no nail salon shots or latte-sipping images. This magazine was for the power brokers, and it covered the deals inked by agents, lawyers, producers, and the money men and women who poured cash into the creations that audiences longed to see. A thrill rushed down my spine as I read the news report.

Oscar-nommed teen star Riley Belle signed the first project under her production company McDoodles. Titled My Life as a Teen Paparazzo, *the film tells the story of a young paparazzo who teams up with a teen private eye and becomes embroiled in a blackmail plot to sabotage an irrevocably bad film. "It's a romantic-comedy mystery and I'm delighted to bring this original story to the screen," Belle said in a statement. The script will be penned by first-time screenwriter Anaka Griffin, daughter of Griffin Studios head, Graham Griffin. He was not involved in the deal. In other news, Avery Brock has been replaced as director of The Weekenders. Chelsea Knox has been nabbed to helm the film, which has suffered script problems for years. Knox said she'll be returning to the original script. "The Weekenders was a classic hit of the last generation and I'm delighted to reintroduce it to the new generation with its original script intact, with one small change. The character played by Riley Belle will eat vegetarian sushi rather than raw fish sushi during her lunch in detention." As a result of the script change, the cast has been whittled down to the original five members of weekend detention. Jenner Davies has been cut from the film.*

Then I headed to class, and crossed my fingers that the employment agency on tap for today would be suitably impressed with William's language skills. I knew I was, in so many ways.

22

Two Months Later
Weather: 70 degrees, Sunny

William

She winced when she saw the open suitcases in my apartment.

"I hate them," she said as she sank down heavily on the couch, tossing her mortarboard on the floor, next to mine. Cruel reminders that we'd crossed such a major milestone together, but *together* was ending in two days. We'd both graduated five days ago. Matthew and Jane and my parents had attended. After the ceremony we all had dinner with Jess, her parents, and her brother and his wife, toasting and celebrating a day I'd been dreading. Graduation was the end of something all right. The end of college. The end of my student visa. The end of us.

True to her word, Jess had been a masterful project manager, overseeing Action Item Number One on her To-Do-List: Get William a Job. I'd had plenty of nibbles, loads of close chances, and so many opportunities in my hands. After Riley had mentioned wanting to expand her next slate of productions globally like other shops were doing, Jess had tracked down a part-time opening at a studio that was importing its TV series to Asia. I'd worked part-time four nights a week teaching basic Japanese to a group of their executives, and the HR manager had loved my work. But the gig was temporary. The executives only needed basic skills, and the studio wasn't committing to full-time employment. Then, the agency that had snubbed me for not having graduated yet called, desperate for help when a translator went on medical leave for knee surgery. But her knee healed in four weeks, and that was the end of my job there.

I'd come up short, and even though I wanted to rail against the system, the fact was this was how the system worked. Finding a permanent job for a non-citizen was phenomenally difficult. You had to have the most unique skills. I had them, but there were simply no openings.

"I hate the suitcases, too," I echoed. "Let's stop looking at them. Maybe if we don't see them, I don't have to go," I said, wishing we could delay the inevitable by ignoring it. Pulling her up from the couch, I led her to my bedroom where I stripped her naked and she did the same for me. I joined her under the covers, tasting the salty streak of her tears as I kissed her while making love to her.

It wouldn't be our last time. I was leaving on Monday, two days from now, and surely there would be many more times. The problem was, I fell deeper in love with her every second I spent with her, and that was going to make Monday suck even harder. The last two months with her had been the best of my life. Not that I had gobs and gobs of years to compare it to, but even at twenty-one, I *knew* a love like this came around once in a blue moon.

Jess

Lying on my side in his bed, I ran my hand down his waist, over his hips, along his thigh. I was memorizing him for later, even though he was imprinted on me. Even without him here, I could close my eyes and picture every muscle and line in his hard body. But in forty-eight hours, memories would be all I had left of him.

We had agreed that it made no sense to continue this long-distance. With med school starting in September, I wasn't going to be in a position to fly to England and visit him on weekends. Nor did I have the kind of spare cash lying around to fund that sort of travel. The money from selling my life story to Riley had covered a full two and a half years of medical school, and that's where every single cent went.

"I'll miss you every day," I said, my voice etched with sadness I didn't even try to mask. I was sad; I was ridiculously sad. I wasn't going to hide it. "Someday, when you're old and married to some fabulous English woman, I hope you'll still look back on me fondly as the girl you fell in love with your last year of college in America."

He pressed a finger to my lips, shushing me. "You will be more than that. And I haven't given up hope. Maybe I'll land a job in London, and I'll request a transfer here in a few months, and we'll be together again."

I shot him a look as if to say *don't be silly*. "That only happens in the movies."

"But you believe in the movies, don't you?" he said, insistent in the possibility that there might be another *us* someday. He was always the dreamer; I was always more practical. I was science; he was words. The statistical probability of *us* working out was slim to none.

"Sure," I said, but my answer sounded noncommittal even to me.

"You never know what fate has in store," he said, then whispered something to me in Italian.

This time I knew what it meant, because he'd taught me. He'd taught me all the things he said when we were making love. His words this time were both beautiful and sexy, and they filled me with joy and sorrow as he told me how much he loved me, more than he's ever loved anyone, more than he ever will, and how he'll miss every inch of me inside and out.

Always.

* * *

Later that night, as I lay awake in his bed, staring out the window, searching for something that wasn't destined to come true, I was blinded with a possibility. Out of nowhere, like a comet tearing through the sky, blasting a message just for me, I knew the answer. I had it with me all along. It had never been far away from me. It had always been a part of me.

I sat up straight, my heart skittering wildly in my chest. I alone had the power to make him stay.

Jess

All through lunch at my parents' house the next day, I could barely concentrate.

Kat and Bryan were here for a farewell meal. They'd stayed in the area after the graduation ceremony, heading to Santa Barbara for a vacation, and they were on their way back to New York tomorrow morning. My mom chatted about why she thought they should find out the genders of the babies at Kat's ultrasound next week. Kat nodded and smiled, then said that she wanted to be surprised at their birth. I hardly listened, because I had only one thing on my mind.

The persistent drumbeat of possibility.

My mom attempted a new angle, suggesting Kat have the ultrasound technician email the genders to *her*, and that way Kat would still be surprised but my mom could still shop for the babies.

Bryan laughed, and clasped his hand over his wife's. "Mom, I think it's Kat's decision in the end."

I had to get away from all this talk of babies, and couples, and the future, because it was clouding my judgment. I had to make this choice free of all the noise, so I pushed back and said, "Excuse me for a minute."

I slipped away from the table, and headed for the backyard, Jennifer close by my side. I slid the glass door shut behind me, and sank down onto a plastic chair on the deck. Jennifer rested her snout on my leg, and I petted her.

The memory of Riley asking her dog for advice flashed before me. Maybe Jennifer had answers.

As I stroked the big dog's nose, I tried Riley's tactic. "Should I do it, Jennifer? I can be the reason he stays. He's never asked me to do this. We've never even talked about it. But are we ready to take that step?"

Jennifer lifted her snout and tilted her head. She revealed no answers.

I sent a text to Jillian.

Jess: *Why can't love be as easy as taking pictures? Wait. I don't want you to know I think taking pictures is easy.*

Jillian: *When you love something, it can feel easy. Also, why is love feeling so hard?*

Jess: *Not so much love, but decisions. I need to make one.*

Jillian: *I have faith in you. You'll make the right ones. You always do.*

But did I? I wasn't so sure. I wanted to make the right ones. I wanted to make the best ones. A creaking sound filled my ears. Kat had opened the door and was sliding it shut behind her.

"Hey, Jess," she said, taking the seat next to me on the deck. "You seemed out of sorts at lunch. Are you okay?"

"No," I said, not bothering to fake it.

"What's wrong? Is it William leaving?"

"Yes," I said, because they all knew the clock was ticking.

"And you're missing him like crazy."

"I am," I said, staring off into the small yard and the wood fence at the edge. I couldn't look at her. I couldn't look at anyone. I needed to find the answer myself. "And I want him to stay."

She shifted her chair, moving closer to me, forcing me to look at her. "So are you going to do it?"

I furrowed my brows. "Do what?"

"Ask him to marry you so he can stay."

My heart nearly stopped and my eyes widened. "Did you hear me talking to the dog?" I asked in a hushed voice.

She shook her head. "No. But it doesn't take a genius to see that you're sad, nor does it take much to figure out that you're trying to make a hard decision."

"But if it's a hard decision, doesn't that mean it's the wrong decision, Kat? I'm only twenty-one. I'm going to med school. Should I really get married now? Do I marry him just so he can stay? Assuming he'd even say yes?"

She smiled sweetly at me. "That's a lot of questions, and I don't have the answers to any except for the last one, and I suspect you know the answer to it as well."

"It just seems wrong to marry him just so he can stay."

"Then don't do it."

"But I can't stand the thought of him leaving. And I have the power to make him stay. All I have to do is go down to the courthouse with him and we say *I do*, and voilà. Instant citizen."

"So do it."

I scoffed. "You're not helpful," I said with a small pout.

"Because marriage isn't an easy decision when it's complicated by factors beyond love. If love was the only reason, then it would be an easy choice."

I slinked down in the chair, sighing heavily. "But if it was meant to be, why did it not even occur to me until last night that I could even do this? I literally never even thought about it or considered it until last night. Then it hit me like that," I said, snapping my fingers. "Why did it never even enter the realm of possibility until last night?"

Kat quirked up her lips, a knowing twinkle in her pretty brown eyes. "Maybe it occurred to you because you were finally ready to consider it. Maybe you never thought about it because it was never something you would do. Maybe the idea came to you because it's what you want?"

"But am I even ready to be married?" I asked, my voice starting to break.

"All I know, Jess, is that love comes around when you least expect it. It has a way of wreaking havoc on your life and your plans and challenging you in ways you never saw coming. But when you meet the person you want to spend the rest of your life with, you'll often upend all your plans." Then her chair legs scratched across the deck. "I need to pee. These babies," she said, patting her belly. She dropped a kiss to my forehead and whispered, "Listen to your heart. The heart knows what's right for you."

She walked inside, leaving me alone with my dog, and my racing thoughts. I closed my eyes and raised my face to the sun, letting the last two months wash over me until it was time to head to the hospital for my volunteer shift.

I leashed up Jennifer and visited the children's ward for the next hour, the visit reminding me that nothing in life was easy.

But one thing *was* easy. Texting William and asking him to meet me here when my shift ended.

Helen peppered me with questions as she walked with me down the hall and to the emergency room exit. "Are they going to let you on the set of *My Life As a Teen Paparazzo* when they start shooting?"

I laughed. "Why? You want a report on all the hot young actors?"

"Duh," she said, rolling her eyes.

"Anaka just finished the first rewrite last week so we're still a ways off."

"Promise me one thing," she said, tucking the papers she was carrying under her elbow.

"Sure."

"You'll snap some photos just for me of the guys."

"Of course, Helen."

"Thank God. I could use a little eye candy in my life. I've been up to my ears in HR paperwork these days."

"Less time to read the gossip rags?" I asked as Jennifer trotted by my side.

"It's killing me," she said in mock desperation. Then she lowered her voice to a whisper. "There's your hottie, and I swear he gets better looking by the day."

I scanned the lobby up ahead, my eyes landing on William as he walked through the door. He did get better looking every day, and my eyes would surely miss looking at his fabulous face. I raised my hand to wave, but then, as fast as a whip, William turned his gaze away from me. As we rounded the corner, the lobby coming into full view, I saw a man crumpled in a chair, bent over at the waist, clutching his belly.

The black-haired man seemed to be wincing, his face screwed up in pain. A nurse was kneeling by his side, her palm resting on his knee, as she shook her head. "I'm sorry, I don't understand you." The nurse spotted Helen and called out. "Helen, where's our

Chinese translator? I think that's the language he's speaking."

"She quit the other day. I haven't found a new one yet. Do you know how hard it is to find someone who knows the language well enough to work in a hospital in Los Angeles?"

The nurse shook her head, shooting the man a rueful look.

Time stopped as I tried to speak, as the bubble of hope inside of me turned into a geyser. I opened my mouth, but before I could say anything, I heard words. Words I didn't know at all. Words that made no earthly sense to me. Spoken with just a sliver of a British accent.

The sun ignited in my chest. A supernova streaked across the sky.

You never know what fate has in store.

William asked more questions as he kneeled next to the man, who looked up with so much pain in his eyes, but some kind of relief, too. Finally, someone understood him. Someone could speak for his pain. The man answered, and William nodded, then asked a few more questions, then nodded again.

Feet planted wide, Helen stood in place, her jaw agape. The nurse stared, dumbstruck. Jennifer wagged her tail. And William alone had the answers they needed. He patted the man gently on the knee, rose, and turned to the ER nurse.

"He said he's had stomach pains on his right side for five days now. They're not going away; they're only intensifying. He was told last week by urgent care that he had a stomach virus, but it's worsened," William explained, and I wanted to jump up and down.

"It's not a stomach virus," I said quickly, answering like I was on a game show. "He has a ruptured appendix."

The nurse's eyes lit up and she shot me a look that said she was impressed. "That's exactly what I was going to say. Let's take him back to see a doctor about a possible emergency appendectomy."

The nurse took two steps toward the patient, then stopped and spoke to Helen. "Wait. What if we need more help translating?"

"Can you work right now?" Helen said to William.

"Yes. I can. Absolutely," he said, as the nurse offered her elbow to the man and helped him up.

"He speaks Japanese, Spanish, and Italian, too," I said, practically bouncing on my toes.

Helen emitted a low whistle of appreciation. "Damn, girl. He's a keeper."

"I know."

"And a keeper for me, too. William, any chance you can work tomorrow, the rest of the week, and into the foreseeable future?"

A wild grin erupted on his face. "Yes."

"Then consider yourself hired."

"That's it?" he asked carefully. "You're hiring me full-time? I don't need an interview?"

"I've never had a more convincing job interview in my life," Helen said.

"You know I'm on a student visa and I'd have to transfer it to a work visa if you can sponsor me for it?"

She waved a hand as if to say *no big deal*. "Been there. Done that. Nothing I can't handle. I'll get moving on all the paperwork right now."

Some things in life were easy, if they were meant to be. Maybe William had run into such trouble with work because this was the job he was meant to have.

I turned to him. "You're staying," I said, and I was ready to jump into his arms, hug him, and smother him in kisses. But there was no time for that because he was clocking in.

"I'm staying," he said, and I'd never seen him look happier in all our days together.

"And to think, I was just about to ask you to marry me so you could stay."

His gray eyes sparkled so brightly they seemed silver. "You were?"

I nodded. "I was."

"I'd have said yes so I could see you every day."

"Good. Now get to work. I'm going to find some musicians to snap photos of now. I'll see you after work," I said.

"I'll see you after work," he echoed, then followed the nurse and the patient into the job that he alone could do.

EPILOGUE

Six Months Later
Weather: 70 degrees, Sunny

<u>Jess</u>

I married him anyway six months later. Sometimes you just know when it's right. Besides, when you meet the person you want to spend the rest of your life with, you'd be stupid to let a little thing like an ocean, or a passport, or a nationality stand between you.

We said *I do* at the L.A County Courthouse. We said it because we wanted to. Not because we had to. But because we were ready.

I wore a white sundress and carried a bouquet of daisies. He wore slacks, a white button-down, and the cuff links I'd given him. The ceremony lasted all of two minutes, and then the justice of the peace pronounced us husband and wife. We signed the marriage certificate, and then we walked out of the courthouse into another perfect day. The sun was dropping in the sky, tipping near the horizon. We were living together now. Anaka had moved into her own place, and William was working hard at the hospital. Medical school was insane, and we didn't see each other much, but we made the most of our time together. We had time together. That was the best part of all.

"You made me an American," he said, holding my hand as we walked down the street.

"You made me happy," I said, squeezing his hand in emphasis, as I smiled at him.

"You've done the same for me."

"There's only one thing we haven't figured out yet, William," I said, as we headed to his motorcycle a few blocks away.

"What's that?"

"Since I'm giving you the thing you want most, I'm going to insist you take my name now that I've made you a citizen."

He laughed. "But that's where you're wrong, Jess. You're what I want most in the world."

"Then you're mine forever, Mr. William Leighton."

"Mrs. Jess Harrigan," he fired back at me.

"We can keep this up for a long time."

"Like, say, forever?"

"Yes, forever," I said, looking at him and loving the playful glint in his eyes.

"Sounds good to me," he said, then stopped walking and pulled me in close. "And now I'm going to kiss my bride."

As the sun began to set, we kissed on the Los Angeles street for a long, long time. When we pulled apart, he smiled that boyish smile I adored. "So what happens next?" he asked.

"I think this is where they roll the credits."

"And after the credits?"

"Nobody knows what happens then," I said.

"We should find out."

"Actually, I think I know what happens."

"What happens?"

"They live happily ever after and eat ice cream."

"Then hop on my bike, wrap your arms around me, and let's go to the ice cream shack."

When we arrived at the beach, I ordered chocolate with a chocolate shell, and took a big bite. It tasted delicious. So good, in fact, that I shared it with my husband.

THE END

If you enjoyed STARS IN THEIR EYES, you'll probably get a kick out of Jillian and Jones' story in MOST LIKELY TO SCORE! This sexy forbidden romance between a star athlete and his publicist is <u>available everywhere!</u>

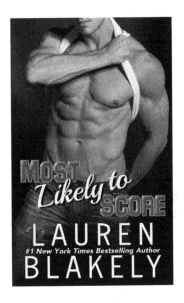

<u>CHAPTER ONE</u>

Jones

I'm buck naked.

I often am.

I'm not an exhibitionist. I simply find I don't have a need for clothes most of the time, unless I'm on the field or at a public appearance. *Obviously.*

Pretty sure I was one of those naked kids. You know the type. Runs around in the sprinkler in his backyard in the buff. Streaks down the hallway with nothing on. Oh wait, that was me in college, too, and I did that stunt on multiple occasions. So often in fact, I was nicknamed Flash. I was fast. Still am. Like a motherfucking silver bullet.

Right now, I'm all in with the birthday suit attire, the costume for the annual *Sporting World* body issue.

Okay, perhaps I'm exaggerating. I do have one thing on—my Adam's fig leaf comes in the form of my hands holding a strategically-placed football to cover the goods.

The pigskin is doing its part to make this photo printable in the magazine, though all the shots of star athletes in this issue are in the nude. A tennis player will lob a ball, the racket covering her breasts and her lunge obscuring other not-safe-for-work parts. A swimmer will glide through crystal waters, the angle ensuring it's not a triple-X centerfold shot.

The photographer with the ponytail and lip piercing snaps pictures of me and asks for a smile.

I oblige.

"Love it," Christine says emphatically, her lips and that metal hoop in the bottom one the only parts of her face visible since the lens covers the rest. "How about a little tough-guy look now?"

Because tough guys hold footballs in front of their junk.

"This is my best badass pose," I say, narrowing my eyes and staring at the camera like I'd stare at the secondary of the Miami Mavericks.

"Oh yes, more of that, right, Jillian?" Christine shouts to the other person here in the studio with us.

That person is Jillian, and she hasn't looked my way since I strolled in here and dropped my drawers. Damn shame.

From her spot leaning against the far wall, the team publicist answers in a crisp, professional tone I know well. "Exactly. We love his tough-guy face."

She doesn't even look up from her phone.

I keep working it for Christine, doing my best to make sure my blue eyes will melt whoever is looking at the picture when the magazine hits newsstands and Internet browsers in another few weeks.

It's an evergreen kind of issue, since the body edition is one of the most popular. Gee, I wonder why. I've no doubt this shot of me with a football for my skivvies will quickly surpass the previous most-searched-for image of yours truly—the game-winning catch I made in the end zone in the Super Bowl two years ago.

But, to be fair, there's another shot of me that's searched for maybe a tiny bit more. I like to pretend that shot doesn't exist.

"The camera loves you," Christine croons as the snap, snap, snap of the lens keeps the rhythm.

"The feeling is entirely mutual," I say, pursing my lips in an over-the-top kiss.

Christine laughs. "You are my favorite ham in all of sports, Jones. That'll be a perfect outtake for our website."

"That's a brilliant idea," Jillian chimes in. "Make sure to send me a copy for social, please."

"Absolutely," Christine answers.

I sneak a peek at the dark-haired woman by the wall, that silky curtain of sleekness framing her face as she smiles a bright, buoyant, outgoing grin at the photographer then drops her head back down.

Damn.

Jillian Moore is one tough nut to crack.

I'm nearly naked in front of her, and she hasn't once looked my way.

As the woman behind the lens shoots another photo with my favorite ball covering my favorite balls, Jillian doesn't even spare another glance.

I'm going to need a whole new playbook to get this woman's attention.

CHAPTER TWO

Jillian

I won't look down.

I repeat my mantra over and over, till it's branded on my brain.

This might very well be my biggest challenge, and I mastered the skill of *eyes up* many years ago.

But now? As I stand in the corner of the photo studio, I'm being tested to my limits.

I'm dying here. Simply dying.

The temptation to ogle Jones is overwhelming, and if there was ever a time to write myself a permission slip to stare, now would be it. An excuse, if you will. For a second or two. That's all.

The man is posing, for crying out loud. He's the center of attention. The lights shine on his statue-of-David physique. Michelangelo would chomp at the bit to sculpt him—carved abs with definition so fine you could scrub your sheets on his washboard, arms that could lift a woman easily and carry her up a flight of stairs before he took her, powerful thighs that suggest unparalleled stamina, and an ass that defies gravity.

I know because I've looked at his photos on many occasions. In the office. Out of the office. On my phone. On the computer.

In every freaking magazine the guy's been in.

It's my job to be aware of the press the players generate.

But it's not my job to check out his photos after hours; however, I partake of that little hobby regularly. He gives my search bar quite a workout.

Still, I won't let myself stare at him in person, not in his current state of undress. My tongue would imitate a cartoon character's and slam to the floor.

If I gawk at him, I'll start crossing lines.

Lines I've mastered as a publicist for an NFL team.

It's something my mentor taught me when I began as an intern at the Renegades seven years ago, straight out of college. Lily Eckles escorted me through the locker room my first day on the job and said, "The best piece of advice I can give you is this: don't ever look down."

I'd furrowed my brow, trying to understand what she meant. Was it some wise, old adage, perhaps an inspirational saying about reaching for the stars?

When she opened the door to the locker room, the true meaning hit me.

Everywhere, there were dicks.

It was a parade of appendages and swinging parts, sticks and balls as far as the eye could see.

The truth of pro ballers is simple—they let it all hang out all the time, and they love it.

So much so that the running joke among the female reporters who cover the team is that with the amount of swagger going on in the locker room when ladies are present, the TV channels should all be renamed the C&B networks.

But when you work with men who train their bodies for hours a day, and then use those same physiques to win championships, you can't be a woman who ogles them in the locker room.

Can you say tacky, trashy, and gauche?

It's not easy, but after all these years with the Renegades, I've learned how to handle the locker room games.

The guys will drop pens.

The guys will drop bandages.

The guys will drop trou.

Astonishingly enough, there's never a need to pick up a pen, a bandage, or a player's pair of pants for them, but they'll ask. Oh yes, will they test anyone with a pair of breasts.

Many women fail.

I've witnessed this initiation of every female reporter who's set foot in the locker room on my watch. Last year, a new gal from an online outlet let her big eyes stray across the entire offensive line. Not only did she get an eyeful of skin and meat, each of the three-hundred-pound-plus linemen did a little dance and shimmy for her. Her face turned beet red, and the next time she appeared in the locker room, all the guys went full synchronized monty, singing, "Take it all off."

She laughed and tried her best to interview them.

But their answers were straight out of the bullshit handbook and became even more ridiculous the more she giggled as they talked. She never earned another assignment to cover the team. They didn't take her seriously after she checked them out.

I love my job, I want to be respected, and I absolutely want to be taken seriously.

That's why I won't even risk looking at Jones's ridiculous body, not now from my spot against the wall in the studio, and not even when the photographer, who I know well from having worked on tons of *Sporting World* spreads with her, lowers her camera and calls me over. "Come see these shots, Jillian. Pretty sure they're the definition of cover-worthy."

That piques my interest. There are never any guarantees which athlete will make it from the pages all the way to the cover, and with a dozen elite stars from all sorts of sports tapped for the shoot, the odds are slim. But the chance to have one of my guys on the cover would be quite a coup for the team. For me, too, since I pitched him for the issue. Not only does he have the body, he has the personality to shine through.

I join her and peer at the back of her Nikon as she

toggles through shot after shot of the sexiest man I've ever seen. My mouth goes dry. A pulse of heat races down my body as I ogle him in the viewfinder. Fine, I'm not unbiased, but I dare anyone to disagree that he's cover-worthy.

"Are any decent? Or do you think we need to shoot the whole round again on account of me being so unphotogenic?" Jones calls out, that deep, rumbly voice tingling over my skin.

"That's true. You really do take awful pictures," I say drily, since he knows he takes nothing of the sort.

"That's what I figured. They're all hideous, no doubt."

I glance at Christine. "You can find a way to Photoshop these and make him look decent, right? Maybe halfway normal?" I ask, a desperate plea in my voice.

Christine laughs. "I'll certainly do my best, but I can't promise anything. I'm not a miracle worker." She winks in his direction, making sure he knows we're kidding.

"That's a shame. Why don't I check them out with you?" Jones suggests in a serious tone, going along with the ruse.

My pulse quickens to rocket speed when I hear him drop the football to the floor with a *thunk*.

Dear Lord, he's naked right now. One hundred percent naked.

Eyes up, eyes up, eyes up.

"I'll just grab my towel," he says, and I breathe a massive sigh of relief. He won't be standing next to me in his naked glory after all. God bless towels so very much.

I glance up from the viewfinder and keep my gaze on Christine, whispering, "These shots are to die for."

Christine gives a knowing smile. "No doubt. I might need some for my personal stash," she says under her breath.

I nudge her. "Naughty girl."

"One of the perks of the job."

Jones strides over to us, and I'm so glad he has that towel around his waist. As he moves next to me to check out the pictures, his bare arm a mere millimeter away making me catch my breath, he shifts something to his shoulders.

I gasp when I realize what he draped on them.

His towel.

His freaking towel is on his shoulders.

Jones Beckett, object of my dirty dreams, is in my personal zone, without a stitch of clothing on.

Christine appears unfazed. I want to know her trick.

I draw a quick, quiet breath, calling on all my reserves as the three of us crowd the camera, admiring this man's ability to pose. "You're the ultimate ham," I tell him, keeping the mood as light as I can.

May he never know he's killing me with his nearness.

"Oink, oink," Jones snorts.

Christine laughs. "I'm sure she means pig with great affection."

"I accept her compliment one hundred percent.

Pigs are fine creatures," he says. I glance up briefly from the small screen, and a bolt of heat runs from my chest down my body as his gaze meets mine. His blue eyes are the color of a lake under the summer sky. His jaw is strong and square. His hair is dark and cut short.

For the briefest of seconds, I'm so damn tempted to let my eyes wander down his pecs to his belly, then lower still. I'm only human. I can't help it. I want to see what was hidden behind the football. But I'll be either disappointed or ecstatic, and since I'll never be able to conduct a thorough investigation of any of his parts, it's best to do what I've practiced for many years. I lift my chin, look away, and review the photos.

Flipping through every gorgeous shot.

"I'm going to go back up this card now," Christine says when we're through and excuses herself to huddle with her laptop in another section of the studio.

It's just Jones and me, some lights, and some equipment. A black cloth hangs on the back wall. All noises echo. I flash him a professional smile and swallow past the dryness in my throat, fixing on my professional demeanor like it's a well-tailored skirt. "Great work today. I'm so glad you could make time to do this issue." As one of our marquee players, the man is in demand, so I need to make sure he knows how grateful I am.

"No need to thank me. It was *all* my pleasure." His eyes darken as he stares at me with something like heat in them, a fire that makes no sense to me. "I hope it was yours, too."

I blink. "I'm sorry. Excuse me?" I've no idea why he's acting this way. Why he's dipping his words in the innuendo fondue more than usual.

He shrugs happily, tugging the towel off his neck. "Just saying, I hope it's not too *hard* for you to have to be here."

"It's not too hard at all," I say, taking my time with each word, so I don't overstep, or read something into nothing. He sounds like he's flirting, but that's his MO. The man has been known to toy with me on many occasions. He's a fun, lovable wiseass, and I need to do my best to always remember that about him—*this* is a game.

"It's not?" He raises an eyebrow, then his gaze drifts downward. "Hmm. I thought it was."

With a deadpan tone, I say, "Nothing hard about being with you. In fact, I'd say it's a veritable barrel of monkeys."

He laughs, running that towel over his head, even though his hair isn't wet. "You know what they say about barrels of monkeys."

"No, what do they say, Jones?"

"They get into monkey business." He turns, tosses the towel to the floor, and strolls away.

Mayday, Mayday. The plane's going down. I'm about to get a full serving of perfect booty in my ocular zone. I snap my gaze to my cell phone. Dear God in heaven, thank you for making phones. Thank you for giving us devices that are useful for distraction at moments like this. As I scroll through my messages as if they're the height of fascinating, I try to figure out what he's doing with his towel games.

Is he baiting me in a brand-new way?

The wheels turn in my brain then pick up speed. Yes. That has to be it.

He's playing reindeer games with me, using a towel and his naked body as the game pieces.

Which makes sense. He's a baller, and these guys are competitive in every single pursuit. But little does he know this valedictorian, summa cum laude girl has 206 competitive bones in her body, too.

I won't bend down. I won't look down, either.

I stare straight at the back of his head and call his name. He swivels around, a question mark in his eyes.

I point to the floor. "Jones. You need to pick up your towel."

"Can you—?"

I shake my head. "Not a football's chance in hell. And please, don't ever insult my intelligence again." I smile. "I've been with the team since the guys invented the drop-the-towel game."

He squares his shoulders, heaves a breath, and walks right up to me, as if he's challenging me to stare at his naked physique.

My chin has never been higher. I might as well be watching the ceiling. All I can see is his face.

When he reaches me, he whispers in a husky, dirty tone, "How's the air up there?"

I smirk. "It's clean. Pure as the driven snow. Now, be a good boy and pick up your towel."

Then I turn around, and I swear all the breath

nearly rushes out of me with relief. I need to get the hell out of the photo studio.

I've had a crush on this man since he joined the team. I might be able to act like a robot thanks to extensive training, but I'm only human. A female human, and my blood is heated to Mercury levels right now.

Must. Cool. Off.

I head to the door in desperate search of a bucket of ice water to stick my whole head in, when my brain snags on something I forgot.

I curse under my breath then square my shoulders, calling out to him, "Jones, I need a picture of you for the team's Facebook page. As part of the body issue promos."

I swear I can feel his satisfied Cheshire cat grin forming behind me.

"You want me in the full monty, too?"

"Put the towel on, jaybird. I'm not posting a nude photo, and I'm not scooping *Sporting World* and showing you holding a ball. Just a simple shot of you here at the photo studio. So put the towel on, and smile for the fans who love you."

"If you insist."

I count to ten, since Lord knows he'll drag out the time it takes to sling a towel around his waist. Then, five more seconds for good measure.

I turn around, and he's decent. I raise my phone, and he preens for the camera, doing walk-like-an-Egyptian poses.

He's such a clown, I can't help but crack up.

"You're a certified goofball," I say, laughing.

"Just trying to entertain the crowd."

"Your crowd of one."

"And that one deserves a great show," he says, then flashes me a grin. The brightest, most winning smile I've seen.

When I post it to our feed later, I know hearts will melt and panties will fly off tonight.

But not mine.

They definitely won't be mine.

MOST LIKELY TO SCORE is <u>available everywhere!</u>

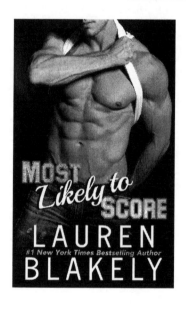

ALSO BY LAUREN BLAKELY

FULL PACKAGE, the #1 New York Times Bestselling romantic comedy!

BIG ROCK, the hit New York Times Bestselling standalone romantic comedy!

MISTER O, also a New York Times Bestselling standalone romantic comedy!

WELL HUNG, a New York Times Bestselling standalone romantic comedy!

JOY RIDE, a USA Today Bestselling standalone romantic comedy!

HARD WOOD, a USA Today Bestselling standalone romantic comedy!

THE SEXY ONE, a New York Times Bestselling bestselling standalone romance!

THE HOT ONE, a USA Today Bestselling bestselling standalone romance!

THE KNOCKED UP PLAN, a multi-week USA Today and Amazon Charts Bestselling bestselling standalone romance!

MOST VALUABLE PLAYBOY, a sexy multi-week USA Today Bestselling sports romance! And its companion sports romance, MOST LIKELY TO SCORE!

THE V CARD, a USA Today Bestselling sinfully sexy romantic comedy!

WANDERLUST, a USA Today Bestselling contemporary romance!

COME AS YOU ARE, a Wall Street Journal and multi-week USA Today Bestselling contemporary romance!

PART-TIME LOVER, a multi-week USA Today Bestselling contemporary romance!

UNBREAK MY HEART, an emotional second chance contemporary romance!

The Heartbreakers! The USA Today and WSJ Bestselling rock star series of standalone!

The New York Times and USA Today Bestselling Seductive Nights series including *Night After Night*, *After This Night*, and *One More Night*

And the two standalone romance novels in the Joy Delivered Duet, *Nights With Him* and Forbidden Nights, both New York Times and USA Today Bestsellers!

Sweet Sinful Nights, Sinful Desire, Sinful Longing and Sinful Love, the complete New York Times Bestselling high-heat romantic suspense series that spins off from *Seductive Nights*!

Playing With Her Heart, a USA Today bestseller, and a sexy Seductive Nights spin-off standalone! (Davis and Jill's romance)

21 Stolen Kisses, the USA Today Bestselling forbidden new adult romance!

Caught Up In Us, a New York Times and USA Today Bestseller! (Kat and Bryan's romance!)

Pretending He's Mine, a Barnes & Noble and iBooks Bestseller! (Reeve & Sutton's romance)

Trophy Husband, a New York Times and USA Today Bestseller! (Chris & McKenna's romance)

Far Too Tempting, the USA Today Bestselling standalone romance! (Matthew and Jane's romance)

My Charming Rival and *My Sexy Rival*
(William and Jess' romance)

My USA Today bestselling No Regrets series that includes
The Thrill of It (Meet Harley and Trey)
and its sequel
Every Second With You

My New York Times and USA Today Bestselling Fighting

Fire series that includes

Burn For Me (Smith and Jamie's romance!)

Melt for Him (Megan and Becker's romance!)

and *Consumed by You* (Travis and Cara's romance!)

The Sapphire Affair series...

The Sapphire Affair

The Sapphire Heist

Out of Bounds

A New York Times Bestselling sexy sports romance

The Only One

A second chance love story!

Stud Finder

A sexy, flirty romance!

CONTACT

I love hearing from readers! You can find me on Twitter at LaurenBlakely3, Instagram at LaurenBlakelyBooks, Facebook at LaurenBlakelyBooks, or online at LaurenBlakely.com. You can also email me at laurenblakelybooks@gmail.com

Made in the USA
Middletown, DE
17 January 2019